Gift of the Ancients

Lightning Strikes

BIANCA D'ARC

Copyright © 2021 Bianca D'Arc
Published by Hawk Publishing, LLC
New York

ISBN-13: 978-1-950196-43-2

The attraction was undeniable, but their timing was atrocious.

Wil and Mandy are both keeping secrets. Wil's is supernatural, Mandy's is more down to earth, but no less devastating. When they meet, both have a common purpose – Wil's father. Mandy was all set to see Wil's dad through his final days, but Wil has another idea in mind.

When undeniable attraction is thwarted by sinister attacks and ghosts from Mandy's past, they must leave the mountain that was Wil's childhood home. Out in the larger world, with help from a team of mercenary shapeshifters, Wil and Mandy discover the truth about their enemies, themselves, and the deep-rooted love that is blossoming between them.

DEDICATION

This one is for my editor, Jess Bimberg, who has been with me since the beginning. She picked *Maiden Flight* out of the slush pile at my former publisher way back in 2005. It was published on Valentine's Day of 2006 – my first-ever romance publication and the start of something bigger than I ever could have imagined.

We've worked together on many of my books, off-and-on, since that time, and especially since I've gone indie, she has been my go-to editor of choice. She *gets* me and my books, which isn't something I can say about all of the editors I've worked with over the years, though there have been many that were quite good. I suspect since Jess was my very first romance editor, she'll always hold a special place of honor.

Thanks, Jess, for always believing in me and my books. Thanks for your patience and your guidance. Thanks for your friendship and your willingness to go the extra mile. You're the best!

And, as always, a special thanks to my family for indulging my many career changes over the years and my crazy imagination.

CHAPTER ONE

"Are you sure you don't need backup?" Liam Kinkaid asked again.

"I'm sure, Lieutenant. My dad's place is at the top of a mountain. We'll see anyone coming a mile away. Plus, I installed sensors the last time I was home. Once we're within the perimeter, I'll get alerts should anyone cross the boundaries I set up," Wil replied. He was feeling edgy as the borrowed SUV bounded up the wood-lined road that led to his father's ranger station in the wilds of Montana.

His dad was on the disabled list—officially—but he still lived at the station, even though his advanced illness made it impossible for him to fulfill the duties of a park ranger. His replacement was living in a trailer the park service had brought in and placed on the property to allow one of their most senior people to die in peace in the home he had lived in for so many years.

Wil's dad had gone home from the hospital to die. That was the earth-shattering truth of the matter. And Wil had known nothing about it until yesterday, when the new park ranger went against his dad's wishes and tracked Wil down to give him the news.

It had taken her a while to break through the military smoke screen surrounding Wil and his elite group of operatives and actually get through to him. He would have to thank her when he finally met the woman. Without her persistence, he wouldn't have had the chance to see his father before the end.

As it was, Wil had brought the unit's doctor, Rick Lovelace, with him, in hopes that Rick might find a way to prolong his dad's life. His commanding officer, Captain Haliwell, had been both supportive and understanding. He'd been willing to detail more of the unit to fly to Montana with Wil, but the base commander on Plum Island where they were currently stationed, Navy Commander Lester Kinkaid, had nixed that idea. Instead, Kinkaid had sent his son, Lieutenant Liam Kinkaid, along with Wil and Rick, hinting that the Naval Lieutenant could smooth the way with any locals they might encounter.

Reading between the lines, Wil realized that Liam, as a lion shapeshifter, could liaise with any other shapeshifters that were in the area.

Apparently, the hinterlands of Montana were prime real estate for shifters.

The existence of shifters was something that Wil and his unit had only just learned about. Their experiences in the ancient city of Babylon and the gifts given to them by a mysterious man in the fabled Tower of Babel had changed their lives forever. As soon as it had become apparent that each man in his unit had gained some sort of extrasensory ability—and that foreign operatives were now hunting them—the Army had stashed them at a Top-Secret base on Plum Island, in the waters off Long Island, in New York.

Long Island was Captain Haliwell's home, so perhaps that had something to do with the decision to put them there, but Wil had to admit the presence of the secret base manned by military shifters was a great place to put a bunch of guys who suddenly had superhero powers. Rick, for example, had gone from being a regular doctor to a man who could heal mortal wounds with nothing but his hands. That had been the first indication that they'd all changed on some inexplicable level.

Wil's own special freak ability hadn't revealed itself until a week or two after they'd all encountered that strange man in the mirage of the Tower of Babel. Wil's particular quirk was that he could now control the weather. He could call lightning and move storms to wherever he wanted them to go. It had taken a while for him to figure out the parameters of his new abilities, but with patience and time—

and encouragement from his teammates—he'd explored a lot of what he could do.

They'd all been sidelined by the Army until the foreign threat could be fully assessed and hopefully dealt with once and for all. They'd been transferred to the command chain that topped out with Admiral Morrow, a fellow who apparently knew all about shifters and other freaks of nature, and deployed them with discretion and care for the U.S. military. It had been his decision to stash them among the shifters on Plum Island, and he'd backed them up the few times they'd been attacked on U.S. soil, covering their tracks and smoothing things over with the locals.

They hadn't been assigned any missions. No, they'd been just living and moving around, doing the normal things you do in life, and they'd been targeted by foreign agents. The attacks had come here in the States, which was a legal problem for them, but Admiral Morrow had fixed things. The most recent bit of action had forced the revelation that their unit was now living on a little island manned almost exclusively by shapeshifters.

The shifters had proven to be good allies with freakish abilities that complemented the superhero powers of Wil's brethren. They'd worked well together, and they'd come to a sort of understanding and camaraderie that he hadn't expected, considering most of them were in the Navy and Wil's unit was Army Special Forces.

What mattered now was that, according to

Liam, there were various groups of shifters in Glacier National Park where Wil's dad lived and had worked until recently. Liam was going to check in with the local leadership and notify them of his presence in the area, which was some kind of courtesy thing. He was also going to alert the local shifters to be on the lookout, just in case the foreign operatives that had been hassling Wil and his unit for the past few months had somehow followed them.

Wil didn't think it would be easy to follow their trail. He had only discovered his father's condition twelve hours before, and the flight out to Montana had been arranged at the last minute. He couldn't really focus on that nebulous threat, right now. The fact that his dad had intended to die alone, without even giving Wil the chance to see him one last time, preyed on his mind.

They rounded the final bend, and the chimney of his dad's cabin showed briefly through the trees. He hadn't been home for a couple of years, but the sight of the old place brought a suspicious moisture to his eyes as it was fully revealed before them.

Liam parked the SUV in front of the cabin and cut the motor. "I'm going to prowl around a bit in the woods before I head back down the mountain," he told Wil while Rick was gathering his gear in the back seat.

Wil nodded, seeing the door of the cabin open, and his father—frail and wasted to skin and bones—shuffled out. He couldn't believe the change in his formerly robust dad. This time, the moisture gathered more quickly, and a tear he couldn't control rolled down his cheek as he met his father's eyes through the window of the SUV.

He couldn't hide in the vehicle all day. It was time to face reality. His dad had been his friend and his self-appointed ass-kicker. He wasn't always an easy man to get along with, but then again, neither was Wil. He'd gotten that personality trait from his old man, which had caused them to clash on some very memorable occasions, but the old coot was still his father, and Wil loved the old guy.

To see him like this broke Wil's heart.

Wil opened the door and got out of the vehicle. He was still dressed in dusty fatigues, as was Rick, who rummaged around in the back of the SUV behind him. Rick was probably being polite, giving Wil a chance to greet his dad in private before intruding on their reunion. Rick was sensitive like that sometimes.

Wil walked up to the cabin's steps and stood there, facing his dad. His dad, who was physically a shadow of the man Wil remembered, though the spark of life remained in his eyes. That spark of fire reassured Wil.

"I didn't expect to see you again, Junior," William Rufus Owens, Senior, said in a thin voice that was weaker than Wil had expected.

"So I gather," Wil said, playing for time. What could he say to his father? His vital, nature-loving dad who had taught him so much about the forest and its creatures.

"I can guess how you found out," Senior

went on, nodding toward the trailer that was parked along one side of the cabin. "That Mandy should've minded her own business," Senior said with surprisingly little heat in his tone. "She's got a soft heart."

"She's persistent, thank heaven," Wil muttered. "I would've come earlier had she been able to track me down," he explained as Rick chose that moment to walk up beside him. "This is my friend, Rick. He's part of my unit, and he has a way with pain management."

Wil stuck to the story they'd concocted on the way here. He suspected his father would reject any sort of medical treatment. After all, that's exactly what he'd done by checking himself out of the hospital and returning home to die on his own terms.

Senior cringed but nodded. "I won't say no to the good drugs, now. I confess to having overestimated my stamina when I left the hospital. Thanks for coming all the way up here, young man," Senior said to Rick, holding out his hand to greet him properly.

Rick stepped closer and took Senior's hand in his. "Rick Lovelace, sir. I've served with your son for several years, now. You can be very proud of his accomplishments. Though, of course, we can't talk about them in detail. Just know that he's done some very important things to keep the world safe from some very bad people."

"I bet you have too, Mr. Lovelace," Senior said, giving Rick a jaunty wink.

Wil noted how Rick held on to Senior's

hand. Touch, Wil knew, was the way Rick was able to diagnose people these days since his super healing ability had kicked in. Rick kept hold of Senior's hand as he mounted the porch steps and then led Senior to one of the chairs. Senior sat, and Rick took the chair next to him, leaving the rarely-used third chair for Wil.

Wil sat after retrieving the duffel bags Rick had left on the ground and stacking them by the door. They had enough gear between them for a few days. The plan was for Rick to make an assessment of Senior's physical state and whether or not he could do anything to help. After that, they'd make further plans.

If there was nothing Rick could do, Wil had been cleared to stay until his father's passing, however long that took. But, on the off chance that Rick could help Senior either recover or, at least, prolong his life, they'd reassess and come up with a workable timeline to present to their captain.

Since the unit wasn't really on call at the moment, they had a little leeway. Admiral Morrow had made it clear that he wanted the unit to figure out what they could do, first, before he'd assign them to any real-world missions. They were in training and under study on Plum Island. Of course, the foreign threat had to be dealt with, as well. Which, for the moment, meant that the men of Wil's unit were well and truly sidelined for the foreseeable future.

Normally, that would have annoyed Wil to no end. He was a man of action, and he hated being shelved when there was work to do. However, right now, this prolonged period of inactivity was a blessing. It meant he could be here with his dad, whatever the outcome of Rick's examination.

Wil took the seat across from his dad and watched him talk with Rick. The old man didn't seem to notice that Rick was still touching him, with one hand on Senior's forearm. Wil watched Rick closely but couldn't discern anything useful. He would have to wait to hear what Rick thought about Senior's condition until they could find a private moment. Wil found himself praying that Rick's news would offer some hope for the old man.

"What happened to your driver?" Senior asked Wil suddenly, drawing Wil's attention back to the current moment.

"Liam," Wil said. "He's a Navy guy and a new friend and ally," he went on. "I got the impression he's never spent much time in the mountains, and it was a long flight. He wanted to stretch his legs and see a bit of the scenery before he heads back down. He has some business down the mountain, but he's staying in the area for a while to be available if we need a ride out."

Was it his imagination or was his father's eyes sparking with even more life than they had before? Wil looked at Rick and caught his teammate's wink and slight grin. Rick was doing something subtle, but Wil had little doubt the new energy and easing of his father's pained expression was Rick's doing.

Did that mean he'd be able to do a whole lot more? Could Rick actually heal Senior's advanced cancer? Wil certainly hoped so. Hell, he more than hoped—he'd been praying for that outcome ever since he'd gotten the news.

Liam chose that moment to appear on the porch. He was so silent he made Wil jump a bit, much to his shame and annoyance. Liam's teasing grin said he knew exactly what he'd done and found it hilarious. Silly cat.

"Beautiful place you have here," Liam commented, looking crisp in his clean fatigues while Wil felt like a rumpled mess. They'd been on the same flight and had taken the same journey, yet the shifter somehow looked like a recruitment poster while Wil showed every mile they'd traveled as if he'd done it all on foot. Liam strode closer and held out his hand to Senior. "You must be Ranger Owens. I'm Liam Kinkaid. Pleasure to meet you, sir."

They shook hands while Wil watched. His father seemed unimpressed by Liam's starch and polish. In fact, Senior looked as if he was sizing Liam up with a suspicious sort of knowledge.

"Nice to meet you, as well, Kinkaid. You going to check in with the local Alpha? He'll be cross if you don't and might let his Pack have a little hunt."

CHAPTER TWO

The shock Wil felt at his father's words was mirrored on Liam's face. It was Rick who laughed, breaking the moment of tension.

"Hot damn," Rick said, drawing everyone's attention. "Not much gets past you, does it, Senior?"

"I'm too old and too sick to beat around the bush. If you two didn't know what he was before now, it was about time you learned," Senior explained with a hint of his old fire.

"You knew about shifters all this time, and you never told me?" Wil asked of his dad.

Senior shook his head. "I've only known for the past few years. There was an incident during one of the wild fires where I was able to save the skin of a young werewolf who'd wandered away from his family at just the wrong time. Since then, I've had a good relationship with the Pack."

"A life debt is a serious thing among my kind," Liam put in.

"They knew I wasn't going to tell anybody. I've lived up here in isolation for decades, and I've known the creatures of this forest just as long. More importantly, they've known me. There was no question I'd betray them once I knew for certain they were more than just wolves." Senior's matter-of-factness about his secret knowledge astounded Wil. "But you're not a wolf," Senior said, his gaze returning to Liam. "Some kind of cat would be my guess, though I know it's rude to ask, so I'm not asking."

"Well, you've got the cat part right," Liam replied, scratching the back of his neck as he shook his head slightly at the odd turn of events. "But my wild side isn't native to this part of the world. More than that, I'm not saying."

Senior nodded. "Understood. Still, you really should check in with the Alpha. He's pretty particular about who and what travels in his territory."

"That was my next stop," Liam said. "I just had to drop these two off first. I was going to ask for the Pack's help in keeping an eye on things if the Alpha proved friendly."

"No worries there. They do a regular security sweep through here a couple times a day. I think they're checking to make sure I haven't kicked the bucket yet." A laugh turned into a wheezy cough that made Wil frown, but Rick didn't seem too concerned. Once the coughing fit had passed, Senior continued, his shrewd eyes focused on all three men, in turn. "Is there some sort of trouble following you? Is that why you need spotters?"

"Never could get much past you, Dad," Wil said, sighing. "It's possible someone might have followed us, though unlikely. Still, it's best to be vigilant."

Wil had never lied to his father about the important things, and he wasn't about to start now. Seeing the light of interest in Senior's weary gaze was good. His dad was intrigued, which might help him fight to stay here, rather than give up and let his spirit move on.

"What sort of trouble have you gotten caught up in, Junior?" his father demanded, gaze narrowing in the way Wil remembered from his teen years.

"Not my fault," Wil claimed, raising both hands palms held outward in innocence. "We got into some action overseas, and recently, we've discovered that a few agents of a foreign government have come after us in retaliation."

He couldn't explain that the foreign agents wanted to capture the men of Wil's unit. He couldn't explain about the superpowers gifted by what could only have been a magical djinn in the ancient Tower of Babel. His dad might know all about shifters, but genies? That was a whole other level of weirdness as far as Wil was concerned.

Still, if Senior had already accepted that

shifters existed, Wil held out the hope that the old man might be receptive to learning Wil's secret, as well. Technically, Wil wasn't supposed to tell anyone about what he could do. He was under orders to keep his new abilities Top Secret. In reality, he would reveal his secret to his dad if he found an opportunity. Senior wasn't about to tell anyone else, and it might be the last secret they would ever share.

"Well, if you suspect trouble is coming this way, I hope you'll give us as much warning as possible. I'm fine with standing my ground here, but I'd want to send Mandy away if there's going to be gunfire. That gal has guts, but I don't want her in danger," Senior insisted.

"Is she out on patrol?" Rick asked.

"More importantly, does she know about my kind, too?" Liam added.

"Yes and no, in that order," Senior quipped, smiling a bit. "Mandy is an innocent soul for all of her abilities. She hasn't been up here that long, and she has her reasons for wanting the solitude of this mountain, so I'll thank you three to keep your distance from her if that's what she wants. She hasn't had an easy life to this point. The Alpha had his people check her out, and she's okay by him. That's all you need to know."

That last bit was directed at Liam, who seemed curious. Then again, Liam always had that curious look about him. It must be a feline thing, Wil thought.

"She's checking on an eagle's nest. A new pair was spotted nearby a few months ago, and they're first-time parents. Mandy's taken a liking to them and has been checking on the eaglets every few days. She's got a camera up in a nearby tree so she can watch over them without being too intrusive. And, before you ask, these eagles are just eagles, though we do have a few of the shifter variety in the neighborhood, so I'm told," Senior added.

"I'd better check in with the local Alpha," Liam said on hearing this. "I've been warned that there are more shifters here than regular folk, but I've never been in this part of the world before."

"You know where to go?" Senior asked, raising one eyebrow at the cat shifter.

"They gave me a time and place," Liam replied, looking at his watch. "And I don't want to be late. Nice meeting you, Ranger Owens. Hope to see you again."

Senior just shook his head. "Give my regards to the Alpha and tell him I might still be here for poker night if he wants to come up and meet my son."

"Will do, sir," Liam replied and nodded to Rick and Wil before heading out. He was in the SUV and headed down the mountain in less than a minute.

"Now, tell me. What is he, really? Do you know?" Senior asked Wil with a twinkle in his eye.

Wil grinned. "I thought you said it was rude to ask."

"It is, if I'd asked him. I'm asking you. You're not a shifter," Senior concluded with an answering grin.

Wil had to chuckle. "Not that I know of," he replied, wondering again how his father would take the news that he had other new abilities that were no less magical.

"Liam is a lion shifter," Rick answered Senior's question. "Biggest damn cat I've ever seen up close. His fangs are as long as my hand." Rick held up his hand for emphasis.

"A lion? You don't say," Senior marveled. "And he's in the military?"

"I'm not sure how much we can tell you about that," Rick said, backing down a bit.

Senior chuckled. "Son, I'm on my way out of this world. I won't be sharing what I know with anyone anytime soon, and even if I did babble, anyone who heard would take it as the ravings of a weak mind, or drugs. The drugs I'm not taking but probably should have accepted when they wanted to give me a supply. Speaking of which…" He turned expectant eyes to Rick.

"I've got a few things in my arsenal that could help you rest," Rick replied, glancing over at his packs that Wil had deposited on the other side of the porch steps.

"A little respite from the pain would be good," Senior replied, and Wil was amazed at his candor. His dad would never have admitted to weakness of any kind in the old days. He must be in a lot of pain to admit wanting relief.

"I can arrange that," Rick said with a compassionate expression on his face. "Why don't we go inside where you can lay down and be comfortable. The painkiller isn't meant to make you sleep, but if you've been running on a certain level of pain for a while, you probably haven't been getting enough downtime. The cessation of the pain will likely give you a chance to catch up on the sleep your body needs to keep fighting."

Rick stood, but Senior's hand shot out to catch Rick's forearm in a surprisingly strong grip. "What's left to fight for? I made my peace with this a long time ago. Seeing my son is an unexpected gift, though I didn't really want you to have to remember me this way, but I've done my time on Earth. I'm ready to move on when the good lord wills it."

Rick gave Senior a penetrating look. "What if I told you it might not be your time to go just yet?"

Senior let go of Rick's arm and scoffed, laughing at Rick's words as he stood. "Son, I've had doctors in two states tell me the truth of the matter." Senior began to shuffle back into the house, and Wil followed, shaking his head at Rick and giving him a subtle hand signal.

They had a lot to discuss before finalizing a battle plan for this particular situation. Getting his dad to sleep would afford them a chance to discuss Rick's impressions and what he thought he might be able to do for Senior medically...and magically. Once Wil knew what Rick thought they were up against, he could decide from there how best to deal with Senior.

The two soldiers followed behind the old park ranger as they entered the house where Wil had grown up. His mother hadn't stayed long, but there were the odd signs of her presence here and there—the old curtains with little butterflies printed on them. Long since faded, but still charming in their way. Her chair. Her magazines on the old bookshelf. Senior hadn't changed a thing in the years since Wil had been away.

Senior didn't stop in the main room but went, instead, into his bedroom. Rick took one of the smaller packs he'd brought along. From inside, he pulled out a bit of medical gear as Senior sat on the side of his bed and watched with interested eyes.

"That's military grade stuff, isn't it?" Senior asked. "I hope you aren't going to get into trouble for misappropriation of supplies."

Wil shook his head. "We're sanctioned by our unit commander, Dad. He sent us here on a government flight."

"Why?" Senior asked, frowning. "Not that I'm not grateful, but why the fuss over one old park ranger?"

"Because we all know you aren't just some old park ranger, sir," Rick replied. "You wrote the book we all studied from when we trained in Special Forces. You're not just Ranger Owens. You're Lieutenant Colonel Owens of the 82nd Airborne. You're a legend, sir, and it's our honor to help you in any way we can."

For the first time in many years, Wil actually saw a flush of color come into his father's cheeks as he strove for a stern expression. The old man had never handled praise very well. His time in the military had left a mark on him that had made him seek the solace of the mountains when he got out. The farther away from people, the happier he was in his retirement from Special Operations. Still, he had a distinguished record, and Rick was right. The old man had written several manuals that were still in use today, including the ultimate guidebook for snipers, which had been his specialty.

"That was all a long time ago," Senior replied in a quiet voice.

"Maybe so, but you know we never leave a man behind. You're one of ours, and we're here to assist in whatever way possible," Rick replied seriously, then smiled. "Now, how about a bit of this, and then, you can rest while we figure out what's for dinner?'

"Mandy will be back before long. She'll be surprised to find you here," Senior warned. "Just go easy on her, okay? She'll recognize Junior from the photos, so he should be her first contact."

"Yes, sir," Rick agreed, nodding as he prepared a shot of painkiller. "Now, just lie back, and I'll get this into you. The relief should be almost immediate."

Senior reclined in the bed, and Wil helped cover him with the quilt that lay folded down near the foot of the bed. It was still chilly here on the mountain, even during the day.

Rick administered the shot, and Wil could see the lines of pain that had shown clearly on his dad's face fade, as if by magic. Maybe Rick was using a little magical whammy, as well as the meds. Wil would have to ask him later, once

Senior was asleep, and they could talk freely.

Rick left the room quietly once the shot was administered and Senior seemed to be more comfortable, giving Wil a few minutes alone with his father. Wil brought the room's simple wooden chair around to sit next to his father's bedside, facing the old man.

"I'm glad you came back before the end," Senior surprised Wil by saying. "I thought I was doing the right thing at first, but as time has passed and I get closer to leaving this world, I regretted that I wouldn't get a chance to see you again. I'm glad Mandy tracked you down."

"I'm glad, too, Dad. I'm only sorry I didn't know sooner." Wil held his dad's hand until the old man fell asleep, then tiptoed out of the room to join Rick in the main part of the cabin.

Rick was busy bringing in the rest of their gear from the porch. When he saw Wil, he threw Wil's duffle bag towards him.

"We can both bunk down in my old room," Wil told Rick. "That'll keep us out of Senior's way if he keeps odd hours."

"Good idea," Rick replied. "Is he asleep?"

Wil nodded, and they adjourned to the porch by unspoken agreement. They would see the female ranger approach from there and be out of earshot should Senior wake up. It was time to learn what Rick had discovered from his examination.

CHAPTER THREE

Wil held his breath until they were both seated on the porch. He didn't have to wait long. Rick got right to the point.

"I think I can cure him, but it'll take multiple treatments, and I have no idea how we're going to explain his miraculous recovery to everyone who knows about his condition," Rick said as Wil's heart soared. "Thing is, he's given up hope. How do you think he'll take the news that he's not going to die just yet? He's a little too shrewd to believe any story we could make up."

Wil paused a moment to think. "He knows about shifters, which totally blows my mind. Maybe he wouldn't be too surprised by our little secrets."

"Possible, though we don't really have

clearance to share that information," Rick reminded him. Wil just gave his friend a raised-eyebrow look, and Rick shook his head. "Yeah, okay. I can see your old man isn't the type you can really hide things from. He's going to figure it out if we do any of our mumbo-jumbo." Rick sighed. "At least he's one of us. We know he had skills and has seen a bit of the real world."

"Probably more than we have, if that's possible," Wil replied. "Though, before today, I never would have expected him to talk about shifters or anything remotely magical. I had no idea he knew about any of that."

"The old boy still has some surprises left. I wouldn't expect anything less of a living Special Forces legend," Rick smiled slightly. "I'm really glad I got to meet him, you know? I've never said it, but I've always admired you for who your father was. It must have been epic growing up here." Rick looked around at the forest that wasn't all that far from the cabin.

"Being on top of this mountain was pretty cool, I have to admit," Wil allowed, "but as a teen, all I wanted to do was get off this blasted rock and see some actual people. Bears and wolves are all well and good, but people intrigued me more."

"I guess I can see that. Living up here in virtual isolation has to be rough on a kid."

"And a wife," Wil said, surprised by the bitterness in his own voice. "My mom couldn't take it, and when she split, she didn't take me with her. She said a boy needed his father and that Senior needed me around more than most.

She claimed I reminded the old man that he wasn't in the jungle fighting wars anymore and that I had to stay here. That it was the best place for me and for my dad. I always figured she just didn't want me around, but I got to see her before she passed, and we had a long talk. She told me that I was the only gift she could give my dad that he would keep. That he would need. I made my peace with her before she died, and I think she finally forgave herself for leaving me behind when she took off for the beach."

"California?" Rick asked.

"Exactly. Surf, sand and people galore. That was her scene, and she made a new start out there. I even have a half-sister that I talk to a few times a year, though we're not close."

"I assume the captain knows about her and has her under surveillance, just in case our enemies try to use her to get to you?" Rick frowned.

"Oh, yeah. It's in my personnel file. The captain knows, and Commander Kinkaid assured me that he has contacts out in California who are keeping an eye on Sunny. He implied that the contacts weren't exactly military. My guess was that they were some kind of shifter, but I didn't ask for specifics. Kinkaid can be scary."

"Your sister's name is Sunny?" Rick asked, looking intrigued.

"Yeah, Mom was a bit of a free spirit. She said she went along with my dad naming me after himself, but when she had my sister, she wanted to give her a happy name that wasn't weighted down with so much history and baggage. Her new husband was happy to go along with her. I could tell, the one time I met him, that he loved her deeply. He'd have done anything she wanted, unlike my old man. Not that Senior didn't try. He was just a little too damaged by his time in service to easily adapt to being a civilian after. When he and my mom were together, he was still heavily in transition from operative to park ranger, and he had a lot to work through before he mellowed."

"I guess I can see that. I know he served during some serious shit. That had to have made an impact," Rick said in a quiet, understanding tone.

Wil nodded. "It did. I didn't understand it when I was younger, but I figured it out pretty quick once I started finding my own place in the world. And, when I joined the military, I understood him better than ever. Especially when I earned my Green Beret. There were more than a few senior officers who had known my dad back in the day, and a couple of them shared what they knew of his past, which helped put a lot of things in perspective for me."

Wil would have said more, but he noticed a park ranger's hat coming closer through the distant trees. He stood up and headed for the porch stairs. He wanted to meet the new ranger as gently as possible, without giving her a fright by hiding in the shadows of the porch.

"Heads up," Wil said quietly to Rick. "If I'm

not mistaken, we're about to encounter the mysterious Ranger Mandy."

"Go for it, Junior," Rick said, not moving from his comfy seat on the porch. "I'll stay here until you explain things to her."

Mandy's day wasn't going quite right. The eagle pair had spotted her and were preparing to attack when she hightailed it out of sight. She hadn't been able to check on the eaglets as she'd hoped, and the long walk had been for naught. She should have just stayed at the cabin with William. Lord knew, the old ranger didn't have that long left to him. She wanted to be there for him if he needed anything.

In fact, her boss had given her a lot of leeway in her duties. The entire ranger staff cared for William and wanted to look out for him. They'd given Mandy the job of seeing to his final days since she'd received some medical training as a first responder before moving into this job. Not that William Owens knew about that part of her background. He'd find out if, and when, he needed her services as a nurse. Until then, she was just the new ranger he was teaching the ropes in his retirement.

She walked out of the forest, hoping to see William on the porch of the old cabin. Instead, she stopped short at the sight of a much younger, much fitter man walking down the porch steps. Her breath caught, and then, her brain started working again. She knew this man's face from the photos she'd seen inside the cabin. This had to be William's son, Wil or

Junior, depending on William's mood.

He was wearing rumpled army fatigues and had dark smudges under his eyes, though they didn't detract from his rugged good looks. Golly! He was even better looking in person than in those photos. Something else she realized as she began walking again—those photographs had been taken when he was much younger than he was, now. He'd filled out a lot since then...in all the right ways.

He had the same deep blue eyes his dad had, though the son's had fewer lines around them and were clear and healthy. Wil stood straight and tall, his six-plus feet and heavily muscled frame imposing, though she didn't feel threatened. William, Senior, must have once looked a lot like this much younger version of himself, but age and illness had stooped the once-proud shoulders and withered his strength away.

Wil, Junior, though, was still in the prime of life, and his chiseled cheekbones fascinated her, as did the slight cleft in his chin and strong jaw. His hair was brown, kissed by the sun to have golden highlights, and his complexion attested to his love of the outdoors with a healthy tan. Even with the smudges of sleep deprivation under his blue eyes, he was still one of the most handsome men she'd ever encountered.

If Mandy didn't have so many hang-ups, she could go for William's son in a big way. A *big* way. As it was, a guy this well put together wasn't going to be interested in her. Not with all the baggage she carried around. Better to just act professional. After all, this was a really tough time for William and his son. This wasn't the time to think about flirtation. Nope. Not at all.

Mandy walked up to the man, stopping a few yards from him. "I expect you're William, Junior," she said, figuring a strong offense was the best defense.

"Yes, ma'am." He looked down, and her eyes were drawn to the streaks of sunlit gold in his brown hair. Damn. He really was just too handsome. Of course, he'd just *ma'amed* her. That counted against him, for sure. "I have to thank you for contacting me. I know the Army didn't make that easy, but I'll be forever grateful for your persistence."

Mandy nodded. "Glad my messages finally got through. How long can you stay?"

"I'm here as long as I'm needed," he replied at once. "My C.O. gave me extended leave."

She was taking that in when a shadow moved on the porch, and she went on alert.

"Excuse me," Junior said, glancing in the direction she was looking. "I didn't come alone. My friend and teammate, Dr. Rick Lovelace, came along to see if there was anything he could do to help."

"Your friend is an M.D.?" Mandy asked. She knew her eyebrows had risen in surprise. "Does your father know? He's a little…uh…hostile toward the profession these days, you know."

"Then, what he doesn't know won't hurt him," Junior replied with a rueful grin. "Thanks for the warning. It didn't come up when we arrived, and Dad's asleep right now after Rick gave him something for pain. I just said Rick had some medical knowledge, and Dad probably surmised he was a combat medic or something, from that."

"Probably," Mandy allowed. "I'm glad you got him to rest. He's awake most nights, now, sitting in the window or on the porch, looking out on the forest. I think he's in a lot more pain than he lets on."

She frowned at the memory of how many times she'd awakened to find old Ranger Owens sitting on his porch in near-freezing temperatures and a giant wolf lounging not too far away. William seemed to have tamed a few of the wild wolves that lived on the mountaintop, but they never came near Mandy. Just William. It was part of the mystery of the old man who was something of a legend in ranger circles.

The second man appeared at the top of the porch steps. He was another handsome fellow. Big and brawny, but though she could appreciate his buff bod and good looks, he didn't really do it for her like Junior did. Of course, she had no business sizing any man up. Not now. Possibly not ever. Which was why she'd chosen to live up here on the top of a mountain in the middle of nowhere.

The second man came down off the porch with an open expression and a spark of interest in his piercing blue eyes, which she did her best to ignore. He stopped beside his friend.

"I'm Rick. I suspect you've got a little

medical training, am I right?" His smile was slow and coaxing. "I noticed the I.V. setup in Ranger Owens' room. You've been giving him fluids?"

"When necessary," she admitted. "He can't always drink enough, so to avoid dehydration, he'll sometimes agree to a saline drip, but very little else. I'm surprised you got him to take any medication at all."

"Well, I can be very persuasive," the doctor claimed, then seemed to laugh at his own words. "Plus, we men sometimes have a hard time showing any signs of weakness in front of a lady. Among our own kind, we tend to cut the crap and admit we're not superman."

"Speak for yourself, Doc," Junior quipped, and both men smiled.

She really didn't want to get too involved with these newcomers, but she felt responsible for William's continued wellbeing. She'd invited his son here, of course, because it was only right that the son be given a chance to say goodbye. William had fought her on it, but she'd done it anyway, behind his back. She had no regrets about her actions.

"I usually cook dinner for William," she told the men. "We eat together, then I head to my own trailer for the night. He doesn't eat much these days, but I try to tempt him with things he likes."

Junior stepped a pace closer and bowed his head. "I really can't thank you enough for taking care of my dad through this. If I'd known…"

"You would have come a lot sooner, I'm sure," she finished for him, feeling a bit uncomfortable with his gratitude.

"That I would have," Junior reassured her. "As it is, we just got here. We can definitely fend for ourselves, but we don't want to interrupt your routine too much. How can we assist with dinner prep?"

He stepped back and headed toward the porch stairs, his entire manner unthreatening and helpful. Mandy felt a little odd about having these two strangers in what she had considered her safe zone, but one of them was William's son. Surely, she could trust him. And the other was also a soldier, like William had been. They were reputed to be men of honor. She'd just have to trust that they would behave honorably with her.

CHAPTER FOUR

Wil was caught off guard by the girl-next-door beauty of Ranger Mandy. He hadn't known what to expect of her, but this young, vibrant, shy woman was altogether intriguing. Her dark hair was shoulder-length and wavy, her eyes a strange hazel color that hinted at secrets and mystery.

Wil had known his share of rangers in his youth, both male and female, young and old. Never before had he been so attracted to one of the *lady rangers*, as his father had called them back in the day.

Of course, this was really not the time to get involved with anyone. Especially not the woman who was more familiar with his father's current condition than anyone else. When Rick did his thing, there would be no way to hide it from Ranger Mandy if he was involved with her. Better he keep his distance and they find a covert way to deal with Senior's miraculous recovery.

First, though, they had to break it to Senior that he was going to live. Wil could already tell that was going to be a complicated conversation.

Wil did his best to appear unthreatening as Ranger Mandy walked past him and up the steps to the house. He followed behind, communicating with Rick via silent gestures that spoke volumes. They agreed to give the female ranger space and to try to keep low profiles, though Wil knew that wasn't going to be easy when they were going to be in such close proximity for a few days...or longer.

It all depended on how long Rick's work took. They'd probably know more after the first real treatment. Wil expected Rick to start at the earliest opportunity. Probably sometime later tonight or tomorrow.

"I was planning on tomato soup and a grilled cheese sandwich for dinner," Mandy said as she went straight or the kitchen area of the main room.

The cabin was arranged in an open floor plan where the main room consisted of living room, dining area and kitchen all in the one space. Across the back wall were three doors. One led to the single bathroom, while the other two were the bedrooms. It was a simple place built for a simple life.

"That sounds great. Can we help?" Rick

offered while Wil came to terms with how comfortable this woman was in his father's home.

He decided to be glad someone else had picked up the slack and stepped in to take care of his dad when he hadn't known the old man had needed help. Even if it did feel weird to see a strange woman cooking in his childhood kitchen.

Rick ended up stirring the soup, which had come from a can, while Wil set the table and Mandy flipped grilled cheese sandwiches on the cast iron griddle. Before too much longer, the simple meal was ready, and Wil went to check on his dad.

Senior met him at the door to his room, already making his slow way toward the dinner table. Wil knew better than to offer assistance. Senior may have mellowed a bit, but Wil could see the iron will that had kept his old man alive this long and decided not to mess with it. Still, he was there to catch his dad, should he stumble. As it should be with family.

Wil cursed himself again. He should have been here long before now. He should have reached out to Senior as soon as he'd returned to the States, instead of just assuming everything was as it always had been. Things had a habit of changing. Wil knew that, now, better than most. He shouldn't have taken his father's habitual good health for granted.

Senior sat at his customary spot at the table with Mandy at his right hand around the square table. Wil took his usual spot on the left, and

Rick sat in the fourth chair that had seldom been filled when Wil had still lived at home. Their remote location meant they didn't receive many guests. Any strangers who came all the way up here were either lost or hiking through on their way to somewhere else. Other rangers would stop in, from time to time, for work purposes, but they had seldom stayed for a meal.

"So, Wil, can you tell me what you've been up to since the last time I saw you?" Senior asked once they'd started eating. "I know you can't give me operational details, but just in general. What parts of the world have you seen lately?"

Wil was happy enough to answer. His dad was experienced enough to be able to fill in the blanks, even if Wil couldn't tell him anything about their actual missions.

"Our last deployment was in the Middle East," Wil answered. "We were sent on a sneak and peek to survey some archaeological sites and found a bit more than we bargained for." That was the understatement of the century, but Senior probably thought they'd been involved in a firefight. The reality of what had happened to them in that desert was a whole lot more interesting.

"Archaeological sites?" Mandy repeated, sounding puzzled. "Why would the military be interested in that sort of thing?"

"Dad might've told you that I majored in archaeology in school," Wil said, knowing what he could and couldn't say about his unit. "Our unit is specialized more than some of the others," he told her. "We have experts in several different disciplines, and we go in when that expertise might be more useful than sending in a less well-rounded group of soldiers. In this case, we were trying to pinpoint where the enemy was hiding in order to preserve as much as we could of the priceless artifacts from the origins of mankind."

"Not that the Taliban left much standing after their purge," Rick put in. "It was downright criminal what those people did to ancient structures that had stood for centuries. Firing RPGs at those ancient Buddhas in Afghanistan and reducing them to rubble." Rick shook his head. "That was disgusting."

"That was decades ago," Wil reminded his friend, then turned back to his explanation. "But that's the kind of thing we were trying to avoid. We went in to mark locations and find out where the enemy was hiding. That much I can tell you without giving away any secrets."

"I remember those kinds of missions," Senior replied, his gaze faraway as he recalled his own stint in the military. "Not that we were focused on preservation of artifacts, per se, but the insertions to locate the enemy. Some of those situations were hair-raising."

"I bet," Rick said enthusiastically. "In our case, we ran across some strangeness, and that caused the concern we told you about earlier."

"That reminds me," Senior said, turning to Mandy. "You let me know the minute you see any strangers wandering around the woods, okay? Make sure you keep your radio on you at all times and take the sat phone with you when you do your rounds. These boys came on the double when Wil finally got your message, but they might have brought some trouble with them. If I give you the order to skedaddle, you do it, Mandy. Understand? You're not a soldier, and we don't want you caught in the crossfire if bad things start to happen up here."

"You're not serious?" Mandy looked and sounded outraged.

Wil shook his head. Why, oh why, had his dad gone off-script like this? Was the illness affecting his mind?

"Dad, that was need-to-know," Wil reminded his father.

"And she needs to know," Senior shot back. "If there's going to be trouble, she needs to realize it and get the hell out of Dodge." He turned back to Mandy. "Please just agree, Amanda. I don't want to be worrying about your safety if the worst should happen."

"I can't believe you would bring violence to your father's doorstep!" Mandy exploded, her rage aimed at Wil. "What in the world were you thinking?"

"I was thinking the chances we were tracked here are extremely low and that I needed to be here, no matter the small chance of danger, because my dad needs me," Wil answered honestly. "If I could have thought of any other way to do this, I would have done it, but we're just playing the cards we were dealt here and making the best of it."

"Besides, between me and Junior here," Rick put in, "we're more than capable."

"And I can still shoot," Senior said, a spark of life in his eyes that would not be denied. "I may not be good for much else, but I can still make my rifle sing."

Wil remembered the hidden storage between his room and his dad's that contained an array of sniper rifles, as well as more common firearms. His dad had amassed quite the collection over his years of service.

"Of that, I have no doubt, sir," Rick said with real admiration. "By all accounts, you're an artist with a rifle. Lord knows, your son here had a high level of expectation surrounding him once people realized whose son he was."

"Really?" Senior looked sharply at Wil. "I'm sorry, son. I guess I never thought about that."

Wil shrugged, touched by his dad's concern. "It was okay. I'm just lucky you taught me everything I know about shooting. I was able to live up to the expectations, though I never managed to break your records."

"Nah, he made his own mark," Rick reported when Wil might have preferred his friend to remain silent. "He avoided breaking your records, but he smashed all the others so that now the name Owens is on almost every line of the sniper record list." Rick chuckled while Senior gave his son a cunning smile.

"That's a comfort," Senior replied finally. "I was starting to think all my lessons had been for naught."

"Not at all," Rick went on. "Wil teaches in

the sniper school when we're not on assignment. He keeps us all sharp in the unit, too."

Senior beamed on hearing that but said nothing. He had eaten most of his sandwich, but the soup was growing cold in the dish. His appetite certainly wasn't what is used to be. Rick and Wil had both eaten two of the sandwiches and a serving of soup, and he knew he was going to be raiding the MREs they'd brought along sometime tonight. It had been a long day of travel, and he was still hungry.

Senior excused himself and headed for his room while Rick and Wil helped Mandy clean up the table and kitchen. When all was done, Rick excused himself to set up their bedrolls in Wil's childhood room, leaving Wil to talk with Mandy. She had made tea, which wasn't Wil's usual after dinner drink, but he didn't mind. He sat at the dining table with her, sipping fragrant herbal tea and knew he was about to hear whatever it was Mandy had on her mind.

"Your dad doesn't have long, you know," Mandy told him, not sugar coating her words one bit.

"I know, but Rick has other ideas," Wil answered, laying the groundwork. Mandy would be the hardest one to deal with should Senior start getting miraculously better.

She just shook her head. "William has seen all the doctors, and they all said the same. I know you probably don't want to hear this, but…"

"Rick is involved in some pretty cutting-edge

stuff. I won't give up until I hear what Rick has to say," Wil told her.

"That's your choice, of course, and for William's sake, I hope there's something your friend can do to help him." She sipped her tea. "You know, probably better than I do, how everything works in this house, but I wanted to let you know about the new solar panel that was installed last fall. It worked fine for a while, but it's been on the blink since the last big snow, and we haven't been able to get anyone up here to fix it. I was able to secure it back to the roof, but the electrical stuff is beyond my skill level. If you have any expertise in such things, maybe you could take a look before you leave. We're running at about seventy percent of full power with the rest of the panels, which is enough most of the time, but in the middle of the night, we run out of power sometimes."

"No problem. I'll take a look at it tomorrow," Wil told her, glad to have something tangible to work on.

She stood from the table and went over to the sink to rinse out her tea mug. "I get up pretty early, but don't be surprised to find your dad out on the porch in the middle of the night. He's had trouble sleeping lately, and sometimes, a giant wolf trots out of the forest and sits with him. They seem to be friends, but I can't get close, so don't freak out if you see it."

Knowing what Wil now knew about the shifters in the area and his father's knowledge of their existence, he had a good idea that the wild wolf was really a werewolf who had taken an interest in Wil's dad. That was comforting. At least the old man had company on those nights when he couldn't sleep because of the illness eating away at his body.

All that would change, though. Rick had already said he could do something. Senior wasn't going to die. At least not of this illness, though it had been a close thing. If Mandy hadn't gotten word to Wil, the outcome would have been very different. And very sad.

She was heading for the door of the cabin when Wil caught up with her. He put out a hand to stop her, and she flinched back from the contact. His eyes narrowed. What had happened to this lovely girl in the past to make her so shy of human contact? He didn't know, but he was determined to find out. Tomorrow. For now, he had a few words to say that couldn't be postponed.

"Sorry," he said, backing off and giving her space. "I just wanted to say thank you. If you hadn't found a way to contact me, I never would have known. My dad is just stubborn enough to have gone to his grave without ever telling me what was going on. I have you to thank for changing things, and I want you to know how deeply I appreciate it."

She looked down, clearly uncomfortable with his gratitude, but eventually, she nodded. "I'm glad my message finally got through to you."

CHAPTER FIVE

Mandy walked the short distance to her trailer in darkness lit only by stars. William had a few lights mounted on the outside of the cabin, but she hadn't bothered putting any of them on since the last big snow when the new solar panel practically flew off the roof. She'd been conserving energy ever since, in case William needed it during his nocturnal wanderings.

She couldn't help but think about William's son. She'd known the son was a soldier, but she hadn't expected him to be so...so...

She couldn't come up with a single word to describe the man she had just met. He was ruggedly handsome, which she'd expected based on his photos and his father's chiseled features. William had been a handsome man in his time, and that strong jaw and high cheekbones persisted, even as illness ravaged his body.

The son was also incredibly fit. He had a warrior's physique, and by that, she thought of gladiators of old, not the chairborne rangers of today's more mechanized military. He was intimidating, and yet, something about his steady presence was reassuring. That thought made her pause. It had been a very long time since a man had been able to convey that sort of feeling where she was concerned.

Since her experiences in her last job, men—especially big men like William, Junior—brought fear to her heart, not comfort. Still, the feeling persisted. There was something incredibly calming about Wil's presence that she hadn't expected to feel. Maybe she was getting better. Maybe being up here in the middle of nowhere was working to ease some of the fears she had developed after the trauma she'd been through.

She almost snorted. Yeah, and maybe pigs would fly over the mountain tomorrow morning, too. Mandy knew she still had an irrational response to most men. Wil's friend, Rick, for example, hadn't left her feeling all warm and fuzzy. He'd spooked her when she'd first seen him, and the old fight-or-flight adrenaline reaction had coursed through her veins.

Dammit! She'd been making progress. Or, at least, she'd thought she had. Being up here with only William and the occasional visitor had been helping her keep the fear reactions down to a minimum. She'd been living an almost-normal life. If living on top of a mountain and seeing more wild animals than people could be considered a normal life.

The fact remained, though, that Wil didn't evoke that same fear response. Why that should be puzzled her. He was big and brawny. Clearly skilled in combat. By all rights, she should be running, screaming, into the night. Instead, she felt calm and almost…relieved…knowing he wasn't far away. She felt like she could depend on him to protect her.

She snorted a little at that thought as she mounted the steps into her trailer. She'd prided herself on being able to handle anything, but one terrible situation had shaken her to her very core. She had been forever changed by violence, and she didn't know who she would be when she finally came to terms with what had happened.

The trauma was long past, now. It had been a year since the events that had changed her life and career path. The physical consequences had been healed within weeks. It was the mental wounds that had continued to haunt her until she'd had to give up the career she'd loved to seek the solace of the mountains.

As she prepared for bed, Mandy went through her safety checks, certain that her weapons were where she habitually kept them while she rested—a handgun under her pillow, another under the bed, and several others stashed around the trailer in places she could reach should she be attacked. The doors and windows were locked, and the trailer was secured for the night. It was a while before she fell asleep, looking out the small window toward the porch of the cabin.

She was a light sleeper, now, and if William came outside, she would probably wake up to spy him on the porch, possibly with the big wolf that came to visit him, sitting nearby. Of course, his son was there, now, and that Rick had gotten William to take some medication for the pain. He might actually sleep tonight, which would be a blessing.

Mandy closed her eyes and tried not to think too hard about the very handsome man who elicited such strange emotions in her. Wil had disturbed her peace, but not in a bad way. He'd made her realize that not every man would make her run in fear. If she wasn't running scared from him, there might just be hope that she could find other people out there—other men—who wouldn't generate that untenable response she'd come to dread.

For the first time in a long time, she had hope that, at some point in the distant future, she might be able to be around people again without losing her nerve.

*

Wil heard his father shuffling in the outer room of the cabin sometime around three a.m. Rick blinked at him from across the small room, also awakened by the unfamiliar sound. They'd bedded down in his old room where Wil had taken the mattress off the twin bed and put it along the far wall. Rick had made up a cozy nest for himself on the old box spring while Wil had done the same with the mattress on the floor. They'd both slept on much harder surfaces over the years, so this was no hardship for either of them.

"I'll go see what's up," Wil said.

"He may be feeling a bit more energetic. I did some preliminary work on him after he fell asleep, but it'll take a lot more before he's cured," Rick said quietly.

Wil paused. "Have I said thank you yet?"

"No thanks necessary, my friend," Rick replied immediately. "You've saved my sorry butt any number of times over the years. I'm just glad I can do something to help."

"Still, this is above and beyond, and I can't thank you enough," Wil told his friend. Rick might technically outrank him, but they'd been friends so long, rank didn't really come into it.

Rick nodded once, and Wil left the room. The main room of the cabin was empty, but Wil knew from what Mandy had told him that his dad liked to sit on the porch in the cold of night. Shrugging into his jacket, Wil followed the old man's invisible trail to find him sitting in one of the wooden chairs, looking out into the darkness. Senior looked up at him when Wil joined him.

"Mind if I join you?" Wil asked quietly, unwilling to disturb the quiet of the night.

"Sorry I woke you," Senior replied as Wil sat in the chair next to him.

"How are you feeling?"

Senior eyed his son suspiciously. "Better than I have in a long time, actually," he replied. "Which makes me wonder what exactly was in that shot your friend gave me."

"It wasn't the shot." Rick's voice came to them from the doorway.

Wil looked at Rick and sent him a questioning glance. The accompanying hand signal asked if he was sure about this, and Rick nodded once.

"Seriously? You're going to use hand signals in front of me?" Senior asked, scoffing. "You know I can understand everything, so why bother?"

Wil felt heat in his cheeks and was glad of the darkness that hid his embarrassment somewhat. "Sorry, Pop. Force of habit."

"So, what's the big secret?" Senior asked as Rick joined them on the porch, sitting down opposite Wil's dad in the remaining wooden chair. "And why don't you want me to know, William?"

There it was, that disapproving dad voice that Wil hadn't heard in a long time. Ah, the nostalgia that tone brought back. Wil almost grinned, but there were serious matters to discuss. He'd think about the old days later.

"It's not that I don't want you to know. I figured you'd find out, sooner or later, though you have to understand, this isn't just my secret. It affects our entire unit, and it's so Top Secret that it's what put us under a new command structure," Wil explained in a low tone, trying to impress upon his father how important this was. "I thought I'd find a way to explain it to you in a day or two, but apparently, Rick has other ideas." Wil shot Rick a questioning glance.

"He has a right to know before we go any further," Rick insisted. "I've been thinking about this since we got here, and I think he has to agree to what I propose. It's his life, you know?"

Wil shook his head. Trust his friend, the doctor, to get all ethical on him. Wil would much rather have had Rick heal Senior first and ask questions later.

"You have something to propose?" Senior asked, looking sharply at Rick. "I admit to being very curious as to what you could want from me. I'm not long for this world, as you know. I doubt there's anything I can do for you in my state."

"But what if you're wrong?" Wil asked his dad quietly. "What if everything you've been told was accurate as far as it went, but we've got something that will change the equation in your favor?"

Senior's eyes narrowed. "I'm listening."

Wil sighed, wondering where to begin. "Let me give you the background first, and then, maybe you'll understand this better. Bear with me. It's a very bizarre story."

"I'm still listening. You know I've seen my share of strangeness. I doubt you'll surprise me by anything you have to say," Senior boasted, making Wil shake his head and grin slightly.

"We'll see about that," Wil replied, then launched into his tale. "Our last real world assignment was to do recon in the area of the ancient city of Babylon. We were doing our thing when we came across something that should not have been there. Structures in a deserted city that became increasingly neater and looked as if they'd just been built. We knew Sadam Hussein had been rebuilding parts of some ancient archaeological sites during his time, but this was different. Then, we came across a large tower in the middle of it all, and we went in. I think we were under some kind of influence already at that point, because we didn't really question the compulsion to climb that tower's stairs until we came out at the top where we found a single turbaned man, sitting on a small rug, as if he were waiting for us."

Will shook his head, remembering. "He was dressed strangely, in rich silks of vibrant colors, and he was friendly, but standoffish at first. He asked us questions, and again, I think we were under a spell or something, because we didn't think it strange. He asked us about the war and what side we were on and what tactics had been used by both sides. We told him things we probably shouldn't have and didn't question it at the time. It was bizarre, like I said. Then, he spoke to each of us in turn and said something different to each in an ancient language I've never heard before. One of our guys was a linguist, and he understood it, he claims. The word spoken to me translates to something like *tempests*, and the word spoken to Rick was *healing*. Our linguist friend heard the word *language*. He was good before, but now, he speaks every language they try on him. And Rick went from being a regular, old-fashioned doctor to a guy who can heal bullet wounds just by touching someone. I've seen it first-hand."

Senior looked from Wil to Rick and back again. "You're making this shit up."

"I'm not, Dad," Wil insisted.

Senior seemed nonplussed, looking at Wil in disbelief. "Prove it," he said quietly, almost as if he was afraid that Wil might do exactly that.

Wil looked out at the night sky. "See those clouds blocking the moon?" Wil asked, pointing. When he was sure his dad was looking, Wil crooked his finger, and the clouds wisped away, at his bidding, allowing the moon's light to shine down on Senior's astonished expression.

Senior looked back at Wil, his expression skeptical. "How'd you do that?"

"Since that last mission, I can control weather. I can call storms or send them away. I can direct lightning. I can gather electrical charge from the atmosphere and zap just about anything I want. Rick's helping me train that particular talent for use in medical applications. He's got a theory that I could be a human defibrillator, given a bit of practice, but I can already use the power to cauterize wounds."

"And I can heal your cancer, Colonel," Rick said softly, speaking directly and matter-of-factly to Wil's dad. "I can't do it quickly, but several sessions over several days should do it.

Wil might even be able to help zap the tumors. I can redirect your own immune system and bolster it with the power I now have. I can sort of reset you to the time before you became ill and make it so that the cancer never comes back. You're not really that old. You'd have a good few decades left to you." Rick paused significantly. "If you want them."

Senior blinked, looking a bit like a deer caught in headlights for a moment. "Want them? What kind of fool wouldn't want to live longer? You bet your ass I want those years!"

Wil felt relief race through his body. Thank heaven, Senior wasn't rejecting the idea.

"But I have to confess to a bit of skepticism. The things you say you can do… It just doesn't seem possible," Senior said, his eyes wide.

"Dad, you're friends with a werewolf. Come on. You know magic is real. This is just a different kind of magic, bestowed on us by one of the ancient djinn in the Tower of Babel." Wil chuckled. It was really a wild tale, and his father deserved to know the rest of it. "The foreign agents who are hunting the entire team are doing so—as near as we can figure—because they believe the gift of the ancients rightly belongs to them. They want to capture us, and…well…we're not sure what the plan is after they get us, but I suspect either they have some idea of how to transfer our magic to someone of their choosing or they think there's some way they can manipulate us into working for them. I'm not sure which, and frankly, I don't like either option, so we're going to continue to evade them, and fight them when we can't evade, for as long as possible. But knowing we're being hunted means we need to do this treatment now, while we still have a little time here before they realize we left the base or where we went."

"Where are you assigned?" Senior asked briskly.

"Plum Island. And that's more than I should have told you, but you're one of us, and you're my dad, so I'm bending just about every rule that normally would apply. There are a whole bunch of military shifters on that island, and us. That was an eye-opener, when we learned about them."

"I bet," Senior commiserated.

CHAPTER SIX

"How about you let me get started?" Rick prompted, reaching to touch Senior's arm where it rested on the arm of the chair. "You two talk and don't mind me."

"I don't have to do anything special?" Senior asked Rick, a frown between his eyes.

"No, sir. At this stage, I'm just trickling energy into your body, waking up your immune cells and getting them ready to do their work. I'm also doing a bit of recon," Rick said, closing his eyes in concentration. "I'm locating all the problem areas and identifying which to tackle in what order. I'm also making mental notes about where Wil might be able to use his unique gifts, because this is a big job, and I won't lie—it's going to tire me out. When I'm recovering, Wil can still be working if I give him proper direction, so we can get this done as quickly as possible, and you can start living again."

"Amazing," Senior breathed after a moment. Wil could tell his father was deeply moved. "I didn't think I would have a life much longer. I'd already made my peace with it all and was ready to check out, but now, you're saying I could live a few more decades?" Senior dropped his chin, and Wil saw the glistening of tears in the moonlight. "You have no idea…" Senior's voice trailed off as emotion got the better of him.

Wil put his hand on his dad's shoulder. "I'm just glad we could do this for you," he said in a low voice. "I wasn't ready to lose you, Dad. Not yet."

They were quiet as Rick worked silently, and both of the Owens men dealt with strong emotions. It was some time before Senior spoke again, but when he did, it was clear he was now thinking forward again. It was a positive sign to Wil's mind, even if there were problems that would have to be dealt with.

"I won't be able to stay here," Senior said with a bit of alarm in his tone. "Everybody I know thinks I'm three-quarters dead already. It would raise too many questions if I was suddenly better," Senior seemed to be thinking aloud.

"You know, you're not that old, even for a human," a voice came to them out of the darkness beyond the porch, and Wil and Rick both jumped.

"Stand down," Senior told them both, chuckling. "It's only Norman, the Alpha of the local wolf Pack. Norm, you S.O.B., you just had to sneak up on a private conversation, didn't you?" The man stepped into the light of the moon, and he wasn't alone. "Who's that with you?"

"That's Liam," Wil said, a bit of disgust in his tone. "Does the term *military secret* mean anything to you, Kinkaid?"

Liam held up both hands as the two newcomers approached closer to the porch, mounting the stairs silently.

"I'm shifter first, military second," Liam claimed. "My father, too. But, as it happens, I called him to get clearance for Alpha Boscoe to be let in on the big secret. It just made sense since the human he's been looking after— Ranger Owens—is about to have a major change happen. The Alpha needed some explanation."

"So, you just figured you'd let him eavesdrop on our conversation, rather than telling him yourself," Rick put in, shaking his head as he resumed his seat and took hold of Senior's arm again. "Nice to meet you, Alpha," Rick added, glancing at the strange man, "but I'm in the middle of something here. I hope you don't mind."

The tall man laughed. "By all means, go ahead with your work. I'm glad to see that my friend, William, is in dedicated hands."

"Good to see you, Norm. Thanks for watching over Mandy and me these past months," Senior said to the man.

The other man nodded once, his expression clearing. "It was my honor. It does my heart good to see you looking better already, but you're right about not being able to stay here," the Alpha wolf pointed out. "There would just be too many questions. You'd need to relocate. Perhaps even fake your own death."

"That's a bit extreme, isn't it?" Senior said, grimacing at the thought.

"Not really, Dad. We could probably localize it. You could just pass away here and leave on a military flight with us. The rest of the world didn't know anything about your condition. Just your coworkers here, who you seldom see in person. It could work," Wil enthused.

"I'd need a way to support myself," Senior said contemplatively.

"You could probably find a new job somewhere else. Maybe as a firearms instructor," Norman said. "I know my Pack would hire you in a flash if we could, but you're right, you need to get away from here to start over."

"I bet my dad, Commander Lester Kinkaid, could find a place for you, sir," Liam volunteered.

"You're Les Kinkaid's boy?" Senior asked, grinning. "That explains a few things. I knew your father years ago. We worked together a couple of times, but I didn't know about shifters and such back then."

Liam nodded politely and went on. "If my dad can't find a solution, then I'm sure Admiral

Morrow will help, as well. He knows all about your son's unit and what his friend Rick can do. He's got oversight over all the *extra-special* Special Forces units. I'm sure he could find something for a man with your skills."

"Morrow? I trained with him when we were both coming up the ranks," Senior revealed. "He was a good guy. I had no idea he knew about this magic stuff, though come to think of it, he was always just a little spooky. That man could do things in water drills that most of his fellow Navy SEALs had real trouble mastering."

"I don't know much about his particular talents," Liam said, "but he's not a shifter. That much I do know. What exactly he *is*, is above my paygrade and on a need-to-know basis. Or so my dad assures me." He snickered in the darkness, his amusement clear.

"You've given me a lot to think about," Senior said. "How soon will this start to show, Lovelace?"

The old tone of command had re-entered Senior's voice, Wil was glad to see. He'd also reverted to using Rick's last name, like the commander he'd been of old. The evidence in his father's change from dying to living brought a tear to Wil's eye.

"As I said, I plan on several treatments over the next few days. I'm going to attack the tumors in order of seriousness. But you should start to see rapid improvement. You may have to do a bit of play-acting when Mandy is around. You know, shuffling your feet and trying to look tired and sick."

"I can probably manage that," Senior said with a roll of his eyes. Wil had to stifle a chuckle.

"This healing is going to be complex and taxing. If Wil helps, it'll go faster and be less draining for me so we can get out of here sooner. The threat level increases the longer we're away from the unit. Not just for us, but for the rest of the team, as well," Rick reminded him.

"You just show me what to do, and I'll do it," Wil replied immediately.

"Excellent," Rick replied, removing his hand over Senior's arm. "Tomorrow, we'll work on that. For now, I've done more to stop the worst of the tumor growth and have begun to reverse the deterioration. I've also spurred on your own immune system to start acting against specific problem areas while you sleep."

"Do I have to do anything?" Senior asked.

"Just sit tight and relax. We're doing all the work, for now," Rick reassured him.

"We'll keep an eye out for intruders in the area," the Alpha volunteered. "Liam explained the danger, and we stand ready to help. William has been a good friend to my Pack, and I'm happy to stand lookout while you heal him."

"That's much appreciated, Alpha," Wil replied. "I'm sorry I didn't know about your people before when I lived here."

"You were always considerate of the wild things in this wood," the Alpha surprised Wil by saying. "We watch over everyone and everything on this mountain and in the surrounding areas. For a human, you were a considerate neighbor, never polluting the wild and not harming any of our animal friends." The Alpha grinned at Wil, and he realized there'd been a whole world hidden in the forest that he'd never known. The concept was a bit mind-boggling.

Liam started and signaled for them all to be quiet. A moment later, a dim light went on in Mandy's trailer.

"We'll be in the forest," Liam said as he and the werewolf leader melted down the porch steps and back into the darkness.

"I'll be in the house, sleeping this off," Rick said quietly, yawning as he got up and went back into the cabin.

"Will she come out here?" Wil asked his dad quietly.

"If the wolf is here, she stays inside, but when he's not and she wakes up in the middle of the night, she usually comes and sits with me until I go back in," Senior told him. "Our Mandy doesn't sleep well at times. Nightmares," Senior growled, saying nothing more about what might cause the woman to have bad dreams.

Wil didn't like the idea that Mandy suffered from nightmares. He wanted to know more, but he also knew it wasn't really his place to pry. Still, something about Ranger Mandy intrigued him more than it probably should. He'd wanted to put his arms around her and tell her everything was going to be all right from almost the first moment he'd seen those lovely, wounded eyes of hers.

It was ridiculous, of course. He didn't know her at all, but something deep inside recognized the fragility of her bluster, the courage in her strong stance. He had no doubt there was a story to why she'd taken a job way up here on the top of an unforgiving mountain. He hadn't earned the right to know it yet—if he ever would.

For one thing, there wasn't going to be time for him to get to know her properly. He had to be in and out of here as quickly as possible. He couldn't get involved with her. Not now. Probably not ever. He had to get back to his unit. There was too much going on in his life to start messing around with women. Even if he had finally met a woman who intrigued him more than any other he could remember encountering.

The attraction was undeniable, but the timing was atrocious.

Mandy woke in a cold sweat from a nightmare that was all too familiar. Out of habit, she looked out her trailer window and saw William sitting in his usual spot on the porch. The new part was the man sitting next to him. Wil was a younger version of William, and it was easy to see the apple hadn't fallen far from the tree with this father and son.

She looked around, but the wolf wasn't in residence tonight. Probably because Wil was there. The wolf only came around when nobody else was with William, as if the wolf was guarding him in those times when he had no human guardian nearby to help him. She didn't know why that fanciful thought had occurred to her, but once it ran through her mind, it wouldn't leave her.

Mandy debated whether or not to go outside and join the two men. If it had just been William, she wouldn't have hesitated. She'd have joined him just to have the company, even if they didn't speak much. After the nightmare, she needed the reassurance of William's presence. He'd helped her so much these past months, though he probably had no idea how calming she found it, just sitting with him in the dark of the night when she couldn't sleep for the nightmares.

But now, Wil was there, too. She didn't want to intrude on the father and son, but she also couldn't face sitting here in the dark trailer by herself after the nightmare specter of her past had visited. She got out of bed and dressed hastily, putting on her jacket and boots before leaving the trailer. William and his son might be impervious to the cold, but she certainly wasn't.

Having company to while away the hours before dawn and banish the ghosts of her past was more important to her, right now, than staying warm inside her trailer. Being alone with her thoughts wasn't as comfortable as she'd hoped it would be when she'd agreed to take this post at the top of a lonely mountain.

Sure, she dealt with hikers and visitors to the park during the day, sometimes. She also monitored the wildlife and helped with projects run by the Forest Service. She had many duties to fill her days, as well as the unofficial task her bosses all knew she was performing in looking after William during his final days.

It was night that was hardest. With no duties to fill her time, she had discovered being all alone in the wilderness wasn't as peaceful as she'd expected. It was at night that her thoughts turned to her past and the things she'd come up here to escape. Only, she hadn't escaped them. She'd brought them with her wherever she went, trapped in her mind that had refused to let it go and get on with her life. She felt stuck in a pattern that wasn't altogether healthy for her peace of mind, but she wasn't entirely sure how to fix that.

She had gotten better, though, over the past couple of months. William's calm presence had helped immeasurably. When they had rough nights and sat together out on the porch of the cabin, they didn't speak much, but just…were. Just sitting there, looking out at the forest night and the occasional creature that scurried or flew into sight, calmed her soul on a level she hadn't fully understood until she'd experienced it. William was a restful soul to be around, even if her heart broke every time she realized how little life he had left.

If anyone deserved to live a longer life, it was him. He was such a good man, and he was a legend among the rangers. Every single ranger she had spoken to since coming here had only good things to say about him, and the stories of her heroism during wildfires, storms and other disasters were legendary. He'd touched so many lives in a positive way in his time. He'd helped complete strangers without any thought of recompense. He'd given of himself, time and time again, putting his life on the line for others—both humans and animals. He was probably the finest man she had ever met.

It seemed supremely unfair that his life should be shortened this way. But cancer didn't play fair. She'd seen it first-hand, having nursed her mother through her final, heartbreaking days. Her mother hadn't deserved to die so young. She'd been so full of life and such a kind soul. She should have had more time here, with Mandy. Maybe then, Mandy's life wouldn't have taken such a terrible turn that had led her here, to this lonely mountain.

Shrugging off the morbid thoughts, Mandy left her trailer and headed for the porch. It wasn't a long distance. Just a few yards, but in the darkness, it felt longer and spookier, somehow.

She nodded to William and his son as she took the empty chair without comment. She'd done this many times over the past several months, keeping vigil in the night with William. There was little need for words as the wind whispered its thoughts through the trees and the creatures of the forest made their individual calls.

Somewhere in the distance, a wolf howled. Mandy thought it might just be *the* wolf. The one that liked to come up here and keep

William company when she wasn't around. Another wolf answered the howl from farther away, communicating with its brother over the long distance. Others joined in. It sounded like the whole pack was out there tonight.

CHAPTER SEVEN

When the wolf song ended long minutes later, William stood up. "I think I can sleep now, after that lullaby," he said in a soft voice. "No, you don't have to go. Junior will stay out here with you and make sure you get back to your trailer safe," he told Mandy when she would have gotten up. "You're as safe with him as you are with me."

"I know that, William," she replied at once, knowing the truth of her words in her heart. She hadn't known him even twenty-four hours yet, but she already felt safer with William's son than she had with anyone, possibly ever. "Sleep well, my friend."

"You, too, Miss Mandy," William replied with the ghost of a smile. "Sweet dreams." He nodded at his son and went back inside the house.

Wil watched after his father, concern clear on his face. "Will he be all right on his own?" he asked in a soft voice that wouldn't carry beyond the two of them.

"Yeah, this is something of a normal routine for us, I'm afraid to say," Mandy admitted, sighing as she looked out over the forest.

"I know what troubles him, but what is it that brings you out of your bed in the middle of the night to sit vigil with an old man?"

Wil's softly spoken question made her pause. Something about the stillness of the night and the quiet competence of the man. Also, the fact that he was basically a stranger whom she would likely never see again after his father passed might've had something to do with her surprising impulse to tell him a bit more about herself. And her past.

"I worked in a large city before I became a ranger," Mandy said, staring out into the darkness. "Some things happened in my last job that...traumatized me, a bit. I thought the isolation here would be good for me, and it has been, but what I've recently discovered is that I could run away from the location of my problems, but they stay with me wherever I go. I carry them in my mind, and they come out at night, in dreams that disturb my sleep. Sitting with your father drives them away. Helping him helps me, as well."

"I'm glad he could do that for you," Wil replied after a moment. "I'm sorry for whatever it is that haunts you. As a soldier, I have some memories like that, myself. I understand."

She thought, maybe, he just might. Then, her heart went out to him. Nobody should have to live with memories of violence like the ones she carried around. She kept her thoughts to herself this time, her gaze focused on the sway of the trees in the breeze.

"Trauma doesn't just go away," Wil went on a few moments later, his voice a calming rumble in the dark. "But there are professionals who can help us deal with the aftermath of events. I hope you'll seek help if you need it, Mandy. There is no shame in it. All the guys in my unit have talked to a mental health professional at one time or another. Nobody gets out of Special Forces unscathed, either physically, mentally, or both." He chuckled softly. "Just look at my dad. Nobody takes a job that puts them on the top of a desolate mountain like this without a darn good reason. For Dad, I think it was all his years in the military. He's never discussed it with me, but I know, back in his day, there wasn't the same mental health support available to soldiers as there is now. Dad dealt with his demons in his own way, which included this job and this house. He did good, necessary work up here, but it was a lonely way to live." Wil looked around, surveying the forest. "I could see doing it for a few years and then passing on the post to someone else, but living up here for so long? That's not something I would want for myself. I mean, I grew up here, and I love the place, but even I couldn't live here for the rest of my life. I'd miss people and civilization a bit too much." He looked over at her. "And pizza. I'd especially miss pizza."

"I can make pizza," she offered, smiling at him tentatively.

"You can? As a non-cook, I find that impressive. Maybe you could last up here by yourself, but for your sake, I hope you can wrestle your personal demons into submission and rejoin the rest of us down in civilization someday." His gentle smile made his words kind, not judgmental.

"I think I'd like that, too," she said finally, "but I don't think it'll be anytime soon. I still have some things to work through."

Wil nodded. "I understand, probably better than you think. While I'm here, if you need someone to talk to…"

"Thanks," she told him, meaning it but thinking the likelihood of her telling him any more than she just had was low to nonexistent.

"You ready to try for more sleep or do you want to stay out here a bit longer?"

"Sleep, I think." She rose and made for the porch stairs, surprised to find Wil at her side.

The man was walking her the few yards to her trailer, which touched her deeply. Such a simple gesture, but so gentlemanly and kind. Wil Owens was definitely a chip off the old block, and a good-hearted man.

They walked slowly toward her trailer door. She felt almost reluctant for this dead-of-night interlude to end. She'd never felt this way when parting with William after a session on the porch looking at the stars. Nope, this was unique to the son. A desire to be in his presence just a little longer, though why that should be, she couldn't figure.

She'd been shy of men ever since the incident that had changed her life. She hadn't wanted to be around the vast majority of them for any longer than she had to be. But with Wil...things were different. She felt safe with him in a way she never had with anyone else, even before the events that had changed her forever. She just plain liked being around him.

She'd only known him a short time, but already, she felt more comfortable around him than seemed possible. Perhaps, it was because she knew his dad so well. Or, perhaps, it was just Wil, himself. She knew he was a soldier and that he did something kind of Top Secret, or some such. William had never been really clear on that, but he'd mentioned that his son was in the Special Forces, once or twice.

Wil had that look about him. He was the epitome of the strong, silent type. He also had an air of quiet competence and an aura of protection that made her feel safe. The middle of the night was probably the time for deep thoughts, but she was just too tired to analyze her reactions any further.

They arrived at her door, and she climbed up the step that hung down from the bottom of the trailer, opening the outer door as she turned to thank Wil for his escort. Coming up short, she found him much closer to her than she'd expected, and the step put her face on level with his. She jumped a bit and might have fallen off the step, but Wil's arm shot around her waist, steadying her.

Her breath came short at the sudden closeness, and the moment stretched…

"It may sound trite, but you're a beautiful woman, Mandy. Too beautiful and kind to lock yourself away up here in the middle of nowhere," he whispered, and she got the impression he really believed what he said. That he really cared.

"Why do I feel as if I've known you a lot longer than just a few hours?" She spoke her thoughts out loud, not censoring them. She'd sort of lost her filter in the year since her trauma.

Wil smiled but didn't let her go. "I thought I was the only one feeling it."

She shook her head slowly, wondering if he really meant what it sounded like he was saying. When the silence went on, and still, he held her, she spoke again.

"I suppose knowing your father, as I do, I feel more comfortable with you. I'm not usually so trusting of men I've just met, but you're a lot like your dad," she whispered. Her breath was making little puffs of cloud in front of her face as the temperature had dropped.

"I'll take that as a compliment," Wil said amiably. Still, he didn't let her go.

She could feel the heat of his body through the layers of her jacket and sweater. He was very warm, and very solid. And so incredibly handsome.

Mandy was struck by her own thoughts. She hadn't thought about a man's appeal like this in a very long time. Not since before she was hurt. She hadn't been attracted to a man since then. Why, all of a sudden, was she feeling this almost magnetic pull toward Wil Owens? What was it about him that made everything as it had been, before her ordeal? Why did she feel so...*normal*...around him, when she hadn't felt normal ever since the attack?

Then, his words repeated in her mind. He'd called her beautiful. He was attracted to her, as well. Confidence she hadn't felt in ages suddenly welled up in her being, and she leaned into Wil, daring greatly to take this moment and savor it. She doubted she'd ever have such a moment again. She would make this one last and cherish it. Hold it close in the time after Wil left the mountain, and she was, once again, alone.

Moving closer, she touched her lips to his.

She thought maybe, at first, she'd surprised him because he didn't seem to move, or even respond. When Mandy would have pulled away, Wil's arm tightened around her waist and pulled her closer, and his lips moved on hers in a real kiss. Her first kiss since her world had blown apart. Perhaps, it would be the last, as well. She didn't really know what her future might hold. Tonight, with this man, under the stars, was her only reality, and she was going to enjoy every last moment.

Looping her arms around his neck, she opened to his seeking tongue, and the kiss deepened into something both steamy and delicious. Her entire body tingled with awareness of this man, in this moment. Nothing else mattered. Not the future. Not the past. Only now.

Wil's kiss was as masterful as the man himself. He took charge, but he didn't overwhelm her—at least, not in a bad way. Her senses might be on overload, but there was no fear, no loss of self, no trauma. It was pure bliss. Heaven brought to Earth in a wet, warm dance of desire that she didn't want to end. Ever.

But, as with all things, it did end. Much too soon, to her way of thinking. Wil drew back by slow degrees but didn't go far, thank goodness. She was so unsteady, she didn't know if she could have stood on her own at that moment. His arm at her waist felt like the only real thing in the world for a few moments as she crashed back to reality amid the cold forest night.

Wil rested his forehead against hers as their breaths mingled in a cloud of frost between them. She noted that she wasn't the only one breathing hard. Good. She wanted him to be as affected by what had just happened as she was. Her feminine pride—which she'd thought had been forever silenced and was happy to find still existed somewhere deep inside—would accept nothing less.

"I'm not really sure what just happened here, but I can't apologize for it," Wil said quietly, drawing back a bit to meet her gaze. He was so handsome in the moonlight, he took her breath away. "You're an intriguing woman, Mandy, and I'm very drawn to you. If only the situation were different." He backed away, releasing her waist, and she felt bereft, though she endeavored to hide her reaction. "But it's not. And I'm not free to get involved with anyone, right now."

"You've got a girlfriend?" she asked, her heart sinking. She hadn't thought William's son was married, but it would be unreasonable to think a guy as wonderful as Wil would be completely unattached.

"No," he replied immediately, shaking his head. "God, no. I'd never have kissed you if I was involved with someone else." He seemed affronted that she would even think such a thing.

She had to smile a bit. "I think you'll find that it was I who kissed you first," she reminded him.

Some devil of amusement had turned this otherwise gut-wrenching moment into something light and rather enjoyable. She felt flirty for the first time in ages. All thanks to Wil. He'd given her back a glimpse of her former self, and it made her feel a bit bubbly inside.

"But you may recall that I took it a bit farther than you probably intended," Wil responded in the same vein, one side of his mouth quirking up in an answering grin.

"Honestly, I don't know what I intended," she told him, sighing. "It was an impulse. A moment. A memory of the girl I used to be."

Damn. She was saying more than she really wanted to reveal. She patted his shoulder and decided a strategic retreat was in order. "Goodnight, Wil. And thanks."

She wouldn't say more. She wouldn't say what she was thanking him for. He didn't need to know what that little kiss had meant to her. He didn't need to know that he had just given her back a piece of herself that she'd thought gone forever.

CHAPTER EIGHT

Wil watched Mandy's trailer door close behind her. She'd scurried away quickly enough, but he still didn't understand exactly what had just happened. One minute, she was climbing the steps. The next, he was kissing her like his life depended on it.

That amazing kiss had felt...big. Life-altering. Earth-moving.

But he couldn't afford to let the earth move for any woman, right now. Not when his life was still so messed up. Not with foreign agents gunning for him and the rest of his unit. Not when he'd been turned into some kind of comic book hero with the ability to control the weather and call lightning down on his enemies.

Sure, some of his buddies had found wives amid the chaos their lives had become, but those women were all special cases. Hal's new wife was literally the girl next door. They had known each other since they were kids and coming back home had meant reuniting with her—someone he already had a special bond with.

One of the other new wives was a veteran, herself. She'd been injured in the line of duty in a far off land. She understood, better than most women ever would, about the kinds of things the unit had seen and done in service to their country. She was a patriot and had seen her share of combat.

The final new, female addition to their tight-knit group had a special power all her own. She'd been able to see the future for many years and had helped the newly-minted seer in their unit to figure out his own powers. They'd paired off. Two peas in a supernatural pod. They were downright spooky when they spoke of the future things they'd seen. Always careful not to give too much detail lest they influence things the wrong way.

Mandy wasn't like those other women. Sure, she had secrets in her past, but she was also more...*normal*, for lack of a better word, than the others. Her situation wasn't supernatural, she wasn't a soldier, and they'd only just met. So, why the hell was he so attracted to her? Why did he keep thinking of her in his future? Why couldn't he let the matter drop and leave the poor woman alone?

What the actual fuck was he doing here? Frustrated, confused, and not knowing what else to do, he ran one hand through his hair in frustration as he turned and headed back to the house. He'd kissed Mandy without thinking, but he'd have to be smarter about things from here on out. He couldn't let that sweet woman get involved any deeper than she already was in his situation. She was here to help his father out, and for that he would be forever grateful, but as far as Wil, himself? It was a definite no-go.

No matter how much his heart argued against his head, he had to be strong. For her sake. He had heard enough hints to understand that something had driven Mandy to the solace of this mountain. Something bad in her past. He wasn't going to put her through more drama by dragging her into his shit show of a life, right now. He had the sense that she'd been through enough already.

The next morning, Senior was feeling markedly better. So much so, that Wil reminded him to "act decrepit" when Mandy was around. That elicited the first real belly laugh he'd heard from his father in a very long time.

Mandy had come and gone while Wil was in the shower. She'd made a large breakfast and placed it on the table, then grabbed a sandwich for herself and headed out, according to his dad.

"Did something happen last night?" Senior asked, one eyebrow arched in that suspicious way Wil remembered well from his teen years.

"I kissed her," Wil admitted, surprising himself with his candor. He wasn't usually the kiss-and-tell type, not even with his buddies in the unit. "Or she kissed me. I'm not really sure how it happened. One minute, she was opening the door to her trailer. The next, she was in my arms."

Senior tried to frown, but the smile in his eyes won out. "All right. It sounds like something spontaneous, and furthermore, it's got her running scared this morning, but not in fear. Judging by the way she kept glancing toward the bathroom door, she was more excited at the prospect of seeing you than afraid of it, so I'll cut you some slack. Thing is," Senior's voice dropped low, and his expression cleared of all humor, "that girl's been hurt bad, and I'm not altogether certain she's ready for any sort of relationship. Besides which, you've got a price on your head, and you won't be here very long." Senior shook his head. "It's a recipe for disaster if you ask me."

"I don't intend to get involved any deeper than I have already, for all the reasons you mentioned," Wil assured his father.

"Still, this is a positive sign that maybe she's starting to come around. She didn't run screaming down the mountain away from you, and even though she's confused this morning, she didn't look unhappy to me. On the contrary," Senior picked up a piece of crisp bacon and nibbled on one end, "she looked happier than I've ever seen her."

"That doesn't really change anything. I'm not in a position to get involved with anyone, right now," Wil told his dad honestly, confused by the entire situation and how it had changed so fast. "Even if I want to."

"So, you do like her?" Senior asked, clearly fishing for information.

"What's not to like? She's smart, pretty, and she's got to have an amazing amount of compassion to come up here and take care of you, like she has," Wil reasoned.

"She's a gentle soul," his father agreed. "But she's got more to her than just that. Mandy is a very complex woman, and you've only seen the tip of the iceberg."

Rick chose that moment to emerge from the bedroom, his hair rumpled on one side where he'd obviously slept hard and long. He yawned as he looked around, scratching his shoulder absently.

"Sorry I overslept," Rick said as he moved into the room. "I sure could use some of that bacon and eggs."

"Using his new skill takes a bit out of him, but sleep and food seems to replenish him easily enough," Wil explained to his dad.

Rick took a seat at the table and wasn't shy about serving himself from the platter Mandy had left in the middle of the table. He was shoveling food into his face at such a rate Wil knew there wouldn't be enough to go around, so he grabbed the frying pan and started frying up a new batch of eggs.

"It does the same thing to most of the unit," Rick said conversationally, between bites, "so I'm not too worried about it. Thing is, it can be a little dangerous for any of us using our skills out in the field if there's no safe place to crash afterward. That's what makes Wil so vital. He can recharge himself, somehow. We've been working on whether or not he can share that energy with others, but so far, it's all experimental."

"Rick," Wil said, a warning in his tone, "that's need-to-know, fella."

Rick rolled his eyes. "Considering who your dad is and how isolated we are up here, with terrorists no doubt on our trail by now, I believe he does need to know."

Wil just shook his head. Rick outranked him, so it was his call, but really, they shouldn't have revealed so much to anyone not cleared by their chain of command. Still, the brass knew who Wil's dad was, and they'd given Rick leave to come with Wil, so they had to have given a few thoughts to the idea that Wil might ask Rick to save his dad's life. They had to know Senior wasn't going to miss a miracle like that happening, and he'd want to know what was going on.

So, in a roundabout way, Wil figured it was okay. Regardless, they'd sort it all out after his dad was well again. Until then, they were playing on borrowed time. Kissing Mandy last night only increased the need for speed. They had to get the job done and get his dad in shape ASAP, then get the hell off this mountain and back to the secure island where the rest of the team waited. Away from the temptation of the luscious Mandy and her wide eyes.

"I was thinking maybe I'd go down the

mountain and get some more supplies," Wil said into the silence that was broken only by Rick's chewing. "Rick and I didn't think too far ahead about provisions when we set out. We're going to run out of food right quick at this rate."

Rick frowned at him. "I don't think either of us should be going anywhere alone, right now. Just in case."

"Mandy's working and won't be back until tonight. Someone should stay with Dad, and it makes sense that it's you, Rick. You can do some easy treatments when you feel up to it and get things moving on the healing. We probably don't have a lot of time if we want to make sure trouble doesn't follow us up here," Wil reminded his partner on this mission. "Plus, I know the area. I can be down to the general store and back in an hour."

They discussed the particulars a bit more, but eventually, Rick went along with Wil's plan. Wil took his dad's four-wheeler out of the old shed behind the house. He could see at once that Mandy had to have been keeping up with the engine, starting it and feeding it oil and gas and whatever other TLC it needed. It started right up when he cranked the engine, and he was off down the trail in no time at all.

The trip down the mountain brought back memories of his youth. Tooling around on a four-wheeler much like this one had been a highlight of his teenage days. There wasn't much civilization in the area, but there was some. A general store halfway down the mountain catered to hikers and campers. On warm summer evenings, Wil would sit outside that old general store and drink soda pop while he talked with visitors about the places they lived and the way their lives were in the big cities and towns and even other countries.

He'd decided early on that when he got old enough, he was going to go places and see things. He hadn't really thought about following in his father's footsteps as a soldier until much later, when he started thinking about how to earn a living and pay for his travels. It didn't take long for him to decide to do his traveling on Uncle Sam's dime, and his dad had already trained him better than most Special Operators. He'd grown up shooting with his dad and qualified as a sharpshooter without even breaking a sweat.

Wil found the old store easily and did a bit of recon before approaching. As far as he could tell, only the usual sort of traffic had come through the area recently. There were no vehicles out front when he parked his dad's four-wheeler near the door, which wasn't unusual. The store saw only sporadic business during the week this time of year.

Wil planned to get provisions, packing as much as he could possibly carry on the back of the four-wheeler. If he had to do another supply run before they left, he would, but hopefully, this haul would last for a few days, even with his dad eating more as he healed.

When Wil entered the general store, it was as if time had stood still. Nothing had changed in the place since he'd been a kid. Mr. Maklin was even still behind the counter, sorting fishing flies. Old man Maklin looked a little grayer and had more wrinkles, but other than that, it was just like old times. He wondered if Mr. Maklin would recognize him.

"Is that you, Junior?" Maklin's grin was a little suspicious, as it always had been when Wil was a kid.

Of course, Macklin remembered him. Wil hadn't changed that much since the last time he'd visited his dad and he'd stopped in for new fishing lures that time and had spent a good half hour talking with Maklin about the old fishing spots and new ones that were even better, according to him.

"Hello, Mr. Maklin. Good to see you." Wil strode forward and greeted the older man with a firm handshake.

"Been expecting you for a while," Maklin's suspicion turned to disapproval.

"It took a while for the message to get through," Wil replied evenly, not rising to Maklin's bait. The old man always liked to rile people up, just to see how they would react. It was all a game to him.

Maklin, seeing he would get no amusement from Wil on that score, seemed to give up. At least, for now. But Wil knew to be on the lookout for an ambush of some kind later, if the opportunity arose. Maklin was a contrary old cuss, but folks around here depended on him for supplies, and he always came through, no matter the weather in these mountains.

"How's Senior today? I expect he hasn't got long, now," Maklin said, not sugar-coating his words. Wil appreciated the old man's frankness.

"He's actually doing pretty well," Wil replied, laying some groundwork in case Maklin came up to see for himself, which had been known to happen on occasion in the past. His dad and the old storekeeper were friends, of a sort. "Thing is, I brought a buddy with me, and I'm afraid we're eating up all the provisions, so I came down to get more."

"You grab what you need, and I'll get some empty boxes. Your dad still have bungee cords on the four-wheeler, or do you need to borrow some?"

"There are plenty on the back, thanks. I'll just load a basket or two. Thanks, Mr. Maklin." Wil went up and down the aisles and filled a couple of baskets, bringing them up to the front counter.

As Maklin was ringing up the groceries he gave Wil another speculative look. *Here it comes*, Will thought. Maklin would try one last time to get a rise out of him before he left the store.

"You know, there were some foreigners in here earlier today, asking if I'd seen you," Maklin declared. Wil had not been expecting *that*.

"What did they look like?" He knew Maklin wouldn't have gossiped about Wil. The old man was loyal to his neighbors.

Maklin slid a couple of sheets of paper across the countertop. "That's them and the car. I got surveillance cameras hooked up to my computer in back," he explained, shocking Wil. "I was going to go up the mountain later and give those to your dad, but since you're here…"

"I'm truly impressed, Mr. Maklin. Thank you." Wil took a quick glance at the photos, but he didn't recognize any of the faces.

"Time stamp is on there," Maklin commented, not stopping his work as he boxed up the groceries for Wil. "I sent 'em over to the east side of the park, but I expect they'll find they're on a wild goose chase sooner or later."

"Hopefully, I'll be long gone by then," Wil muttered. "These folks are dangerous, Mr. Maklin. If you see them in the area again, your best bet is to close up shop and go fishing for a few days."

"You in trouble with the mob, son?" Maklin asked, causing Wil to bust out laughing.

"No, sir," Wil replied when he could speak again. "I can't say too much, you understand, but you know I followed in my daddy's footsteps career-wise."

"He showed me your service portrait and was eager to point out the paratrooper pin and Green Beret," Maklin allowed. "You still in the service?"

"I am. As is the buddy who came with me on this trip. He's got medical skills, and I asked him to come and take a look at Dad. There's no one I trust more when it comes to healing," Wil replied honestly. "We have to get back, but these guys are a bit of leftover business from a recent mission we were on in foreign lands for Uncle Sam."

"Are you saying they're terrorists?" Maklin paused in his packing to meet Wil's gaze.

Wil tilted his head. "More like foreign agents trying to get even with my unit."

Maklin shook his head and finished packing the box. "Well, you know what you're doing, I suppose," the old man muttered, then quoted the total for the groceries.

Wil paid the man and brought the box out to the four-wheeler, securing it with the bungee cords. Hightailing it back up the mountain, Wil knew his deadline for leaving the area had just moved up appreciably.

CHAPTER NINE

When he arrived back at the cabin, he found his dad and Rick sitting quietly on the porch. Rick had his hand casually touching Senior's arm, and Wil recognized that Rick was doing a healing session.

Not wanting to disturb them, he said hello quietly and went about unloading the groceries and putting them away. There was still time to break the bad news, thanks to Mr. Maklin's gift for misdirection.

Wil set about making lunch. He was halfway through cooking when Mandy walked into the cabin.

"I didn't realize..." she started, then trailed off. Wil looked over at her, catching a bit of dismay on her lovely face before she hid it. "Sorry. I usually come back and make lunch for

William," she said.

"While we're here, I don't expect you to have to cook for me and Rick. We're big boys. We can fend for ourselves," he teased, hoping to ease her discomfort. "Consider this a little respite from your caretaking. I bet you haven't had a break from my dad since you came up here."

"I haven't, but I don't mind. Your dad's a great guy."

"That he is," Wil agreed, "but you still don't have to wait on me or Rick. In fact, I'd prefer to wait on you a little. Consider it a little thank you for everything you've done for my dad." He flipped the burgers on the old iron griddle and smiled at her. "How would you like your burger cooked? You look like a medium-well gal to me."

"I do, huh?" Mandy grinned at him. "As a matter of fact, make mine extra well done, if you don't mind."

Wil feigned surprise. "I can't believe I got that wrong, but your wish is my command."

"I'll set the table," Mandy volunteered, moving closer to get the plates down from the cupboard next to the stove.

The four of them ate together, and Wil was proud of his dad's acting ability. He was pretending to be much more fragile than he was feeling. Wil could tell, but he thought Mandy was completely taken in. Rick, on the other hand, was definitely looking tired.

When they were done with the meal, Mandy took off to do her work for the afternoon, and it was finally time for Wil to tell the other men what he'd learned from Maklin. Senior took the news with grim determination and studied the photos Maklin had printed out from his security system.

"We should get copies of these to the Alpha," Senior muttered as he looked at the images.

"I can text them to Liam," Rick volunteered, taking the hard copies and whipping out his phone to take digital images of the printed photos. "This won't be super high quality, but maybe the locals can get originals from the shopkeeper or something, if needed. At least this will give them something to start with."

"How's the security set up, Dad?" Wil asked. "Any changes since I was last here?"

"I have sensors around the perimeter, of course," Senior said. "The ones you installed last time you were here. No updates since then, I'm sorry to say. I have to confess, in the past few months, I haven't kept up with anything. I figured it was over for me, and I let a lot of things that had mattered before fall by the wayside."

"Perfectly understandable, sir," Rick allowed. "Confronting mortality has a way of bringing what matters most into sharper focus." Rick frowned and looked at Wil. "We're going to have to move up the timeline for treatment, which means, you're going to have to help a bit more."

Wil nodded. He wasn't too sure about using his abilities in such a fine-tuned way with so little practice, but he wasn't about to let his insecurities show to his father. As far as Senior was concerned, this was just going to be a walk in the park.

Make that a hike uphill, through three feet of snow, with a ninety-pound rucksack on your back. Piece of cake. Right?

They set to work that afternoon, with Rick guiding Wil's newest skill while Senior sat quietly, watching the forest. For best results, they were out on the porch, where Wil could see the sky and draw on the electric currents he could feel, now that he'd been changed, coursing on the winds. He drew the clouds closer to the mountain top in order to make his work easier. All that water vapor rubbing around up there in the sky created a tangible current he could use.

It wasn't the fierce tumult of a lightning storm, but for this fine work, this subtle energy was much better. Wil and Rick had experimented with this kind of thing back on Plum Island, but they'd never put it to work on something like Senior's tumors. Not to this extent, anyway.

There had been a half-feral housecat Wil had practiced on, with the owner's consent. He'd never felt better than he had when he'd saved that stubborn tomcat from the tumors that had been slowly killing it. The cat had belonged to one of the female shifters on the base, and he'd been gratified by the stoic woman's tears when she realized her beloved animal companion would live a lot longer, healthier life.

Rick coached Wil now, as he had then, talking Wil through the painstaking work of directing that energy he gathered from the atmosphere to where it would do the most good. Rick was able to save his healing energy while Wil did all the work, which meant Senior's healing was progressing at double time.

Wil finished with a particularly difficult spot and sat back. Rick patted him on the shoulder.

"I can see what you're doing, and it's good work. Rest for a minute before we go again," Rick advised. "How are you feeling, sir?" he asked Senior.

"Feeling good," came the prompt reply. Senior's voice was even growing stronger, the more treatment he received. "But I'm concerned about you boys. If the bad guys show up and you're both down for the count, there'll be trouble. Especially you, Rick. Shouldn't you rest while Wil works and vice versa?"

"I'm not actually doing anything, right now," Rick explained. "The passive scan that's sort of always on now for me doesn't really use my internal energy. I just can always tell by touching someone's hand, what's going on inside, in minute detail."

"I don't claim to understand what happened to you boys out in the desert, but that's some nifty trick you have there. Must be hard to live with, though," Senior observed. "After we finish here, I think it's time we opened up the arsenal. You two didn't bring much gear with you, but I've got you covered for weapons and gadgets. They might be a little older than you're used to, but they still work."

Wil perked up. His father seldom allowed anybody else to delve into his private collection of firearms and surveillance gear.

"Why don't we do that now, before Wil does any more work? I think we'd both feel better armed more fully before we go much further," Rick said, standing from his seat on the porch. "We can't be sure how much time we have before trouble catches up to us."

Senior nodded and rose from his seat as well, leaving Wil to follow. They all went into the cabin and right up to the wall between Senior's bedroom and the bathroom.

Opening a secret panel that hid a keypad, Senior punched in the code, and a hidden door clicked open. There was just enough room for all three of them to walk into the long hall-like safe room that housed an honest-to-God arsenal on all three walls.

There were multiple handguns in every caliber, shotguns, assault rifles, sniper rifles, night vision gear, a plethora of scopes, and all sorts of surveillance gizmos. There was even a grenade launcher, though how Senior had gotten his hands on that, Wil didn't know. Plus boxes and boxes of ammo of every shape and size to fit all the firearms. It was a doozy of a collection that had grown since the last time Wil had seen it.

"I had it all set to leave you all this in my will," Senior said, walking on his own with much a much-improved gait. "Mandy would move into the cabin, of course. It's state land, and I don't actually own the place, but I'd arranged with her, and the park service, to allow you time to move my stuff out. I'd even made provision if you couldn't be found within a reasonable timeframe, for all my stuff to be put in storage for you."

"We're going to have to make some decisions soon, Dad, about where you go from here. I don't think a miraculous recovery is going to go down well with everyone who's seen you over the past few months," Wil said, broaching the subject that had been on his mind.

"Well, I've been thinking about that young Navy guy's offer to talk to Lester Kinkaid. Maybe I'll go back with you and see if I can get an appointment with him." Wil was surprised that Senior would be so willing to leave his mountain, but Wil really liked the idea.

"I think that's a great idea, Dad," Wil said, feeling relief flow through his mind.

Wil didn't want the bad guys to go after Senior as a way to get to Wil. Now that they knew of his existence, Senior wasn't really safe up here. Not anymore.

"Plenty of room on our transport for one more," Rick added, smiling at Senior. "This is one hell of a collection, Colonel Owens."

They talked guns while each man selected their weapons of choice and its associated gear. Wil felt better as he strapped on the shoulder holster that corresponded to the Glock he'd borrowed. While his dad went, predictably, for his favorite sniper rifles, both Wil and Rick opted for smaller assault rifles. If they were attacked here, Rick and Wil would be mobile while Senior would likely be taking stationary shots from a limited number of points.

"I think we have time for one more session with Wil before dinner," Rick said as they exited the armory and Senior resealed the hidden door. "Then, I'll do another after dinner and crash. Wil can take first watch, and I should be good to go for second."

"Sounds like a plan," Wil agreed.

All went well. Perhaps even better than expected. Rick said the second session had done even more than the first in eradicating most of the larger tumors. The only side effect was that Senior had to make more frequent trips to the bathroom as his body eliminated the dead cells that had caused so much trouble. Rick had instructed Senior to drink a lot of extra water, as well, which contributed to the flush of his system.

Rick and Wil made dinner, and Mandy joined them around the dining table but left soon after dinner was over and the dishes cleared. Wil supposed she was running scared a bit, after what had happened between them last night, but it worked out for the best. She was in her trailer when Rick sat next to Senior in the living room and did another healing session. This was the longest yet, and after it, Senior looked like a totally different man from the one they'd seen when they'd first arrived.

He was progressing by leaps and bounds due

to the accelerated healing schedule. Liam stopped by around midnight, padding silently up to the cabin as if he'd just materialized from the forest. Wil saw him and opened the door to the cabin without comment. They both knew that Liam wouldn't have just sauntered up if he'd sensed any threat out in the forest. Likewise, Liam had to realize that either Wil or Rick would be on watch.

Liam entered the darkened cabin and navigated in the dark as well as if he'd been wearing night vision gear. That must be handy, Wil thought, to have such good natural night vision. Wil might have other tricks up his sleeve now, but the idea of having animal senses was still pretty impressive.

"Foreigners in the area," Liam commented once he was seated at the dining table where Wil had set up his surveillance post. He had a low-light monitor showing several different infrared camera views of the outside of the cabin and the surrounding forest. "Not tourists, according to the wolves. Acting suspiciously."

"I heard as much this morning from the old man who runs the general store down the mountain," Wil confirmed. "He sent them to the other side of the park." Wil cracked a small smile at what old man Maklin had done.

"How'd you manage that?" Liam asked, looking impressed.

"He did it on his own. Generally, the few locals who live and work around here know my dad and don't like nosey strangers who obviously aren't here for the natural wonder of the place."

"Never realized humans could be so sensitive," Liam said, tilting his head in a very cat-like way.

"Give us a chance. We might surprise you," Wil quipped, smiling at his new shifter friend.

"You're not exactly human anymore, though, are you?" Liam shot back.

"Touché," Wil agreed, nodding once.

"How's it going with your dad?" Liam asked quietly, changing the subject slightly.

"Rick says he's responding really well, and I can easily see the difference in him. I think he's going to come with us when we bug out of here. There would be way too many questions otherwise regarding his amazing recovery. Can you arrange for him to talk to your father tomorrow sometime, on the sat phone, if we don't have to leave sooner?"

"Sure. I think we'll have at least one more day before your hunters catch up with you," Liam said. "The humans did you a solid today. The wolves will run interference tomorrow. If your hunters are merely human—and even if they're not—the wolf Pack up here should be able to keep them occupied. I'll come by around lunch time in the Jeep. Oh, and you've got an array of Pack members guarding the perimeter about a hundred yards out in every direction. They really like your old man," Liam said, shaking his head as a smile touched his lips. "And, of course, I'm on night watch, as well. I know you and Rick are doing guard duty up here, but just know that, if you hear howling, it's them. You'll be able to tell if it's an alarm or just friendly greetings by the frequency and intensity of the calls." Liam stood.

"Thanks, Kinkaid," Wil said, rising also. He offered his hand to the lion shifter, and they shook. "I definitely owe you for all your help here. I mean that."

"Well, if I ever need someone to smite my enemies with lightning, I'll let you know." Liam's chuckle brought an answering grin to Wil's face. It was good to be able to joke about the incredible power that had changed Wil's life so much.

"I'm your guy for smiting," Wil agreed easily as Liam headed out the door, and Wil went back to his post at the table.

CHAPTER TEN

Rick slept right through the time he was supposed to come on watch, but Wil figured he'd let the doctor sleep. He could literally pull energy from the air, and it kept him going, which was a handy skill to have for a soldier. They'd tested it a bit on Plum Island, but this was the first real world test of Wil's new ability, and so far, it was going even better than he'd expected.

When Senior emerged from his room at about four in the morning, he merely waved at Wil before heading out onto the porch. Wil joined him out there, sitting quietly at his side.

"If you go back east with us when we leave, you probably won't ever be able to come back here," Wil said quietly, broaching a subject that had been bothering him.

"Honestly, I've been hiding up here a little too long," Senior surprised him by answering. "I love it. Don't get me wrong. But the prospect of being fit again and able to do things and, perhaps, make a difference to the younger generation has a lot of appeal. I thought I was dead, and now, new opportunities are presenting themselves. It's a little mind-boggling."

"I asked Liam to set up a call with his dad for you later today. Maybe you can firm up some plans with Commander Kinkaid. That might help," Wil offered.

"The will definitely help," Senior agreed. "If I know a bit more about what I'm moving toward, it might be a little easier to leave this behind."

"You know, we could make up some kind of story," Wil said quietly, gauging his dad's reaction. "Like, maybe I'm taking you for experimental treatment or something. In due course, you could be cured and come back. It'll have to be after we neutralize the foreign threat, though."

It went without saying that his unit would deal with the folks who were making their lives so difficult, right now. It was just a matter of time.

"It's a possibility worth considering," Senior replied, "but I don't think I could stay here long. Maybe just visit. If I stayed, the doctors who have been treating me up to this point might get wind of my miracle and want to know the particulars."

"Good point." Wil frowned.

"It'll all work out," Senior said, surprising Wil with his positive attitude. "I'll talk to Lester later today, and we'll figure something out. He always was a good strategist. I'm sure he'll have some ideas."

Senior perked up as Mandy's trailer door opened. She was up again, in the middle of the night, and coming out to join them on the porch. The conversation would have to switch to less volatile topics, but that didn't bother Wil. No, the little alarm bells were going off in his head because he found himself looking forward to her presence just a little too much.

Nothing could come of the attraction he felt towards her. He was already planning to bug out of here as soon as his dad was fit enough to travel. So, why then, was he getting all riled up at the thought of seeing her again? Spending time with her…even if it was just sitting on the porch with his dear old dad around as chaperone.

Mandy joined them, nodding greetings to them both.

"Can't sleep?" Senior asked, his voice pitched low.

"Just some troublesome dreams. Nothing new," Mandy replied, sounding very tired to Wil's ears. Poor woman had nightmares about something. He recognized PTSD when he saw it.

"I get those too, sometimes," he told her, trying not to make too big a deal out of it, lest he upset her, but wanting her to know that she wasn't alone.

Wil didn't know the particulars of what had happened to her, but he was becoming more and more convinced that something bad had occurred in her in life. Something so bad, it had driven her to take this job in the middle of nowhere with only a dying man for company. He shuddered to think of what it could have been.

"I'm going back in," Senior said, rising abruptly from his seat. "You two stay and watch the sun rise. It'll be up in another few minutes." The old devil accompanied his words with a subtle hand gesture that only Wil could see, basically ordering him to stay.

Wil watched his dad go into the house, noting that his walking was much steadier. He'd have to remind Senior to act a bit more decrepit.

"You're really good for him. He's a different man since you've been here," Mandy observed in a soft voice once the door was closed behind Senior. "He's got a lot more color in his cheeks, and he looks better than I've ever seen him."

Unsure what to say, Wil sorted through his possible responses. Denial was probably best, but for some reason, he found it hard to lie to Mandy. Something about her made him want to tell her the truth at all times. He didn't want there to be subterfuge between them.

Those blasted warning bells went off again in his mind as he opened his mouth, but he didn't care. Something else was driving him now. Something more primitive and instinctual.

"Rick's been trying a few things. He's studied around the world and has learned all types of medicine. He takes a slightly different approach than traditional Western doctors." Talk about an understatement.

"Perhaps," Mandy allowed, looking over at him as the first rays of the sun kissed her lovely face. "I think it's you, though. Having his son here has helped his morale. It was kind of you to come all this way to say goodbye. I know it means a lot more to him than he's willing to admit."

He wasn't sure what to say. Again. Mandy kept having that effect on him. So, he changed the topic slightly.

"How did you expect this all to play out? Were you going to be here with him until the end? Did the park service people have any contingency plans?" Wil asked.

"A nurse comes up once a week to talk to your dad, but he always declines medication. He made his wishes clear a while back that he wasn't going to die in a hospital. You probably know Mr. Buchanon, the man in charge of the park. He's got a lot of respect for your dad, and he let me know when I took on this post that I'd be sharing it with your dad for as long as your dad had life in his body." Mandy smiled sadly. "Once I got to know your father, I came to understand his viewpoint about wanting to leave this world on his own terms. I respect his choices, and I told him I'd stay with him, no matter what."

Wil was deeply moved by her compassion.

"And after..." He couldn't say the words. Not even now that he knew the worst wasn't going to happen—at least not for a good long while yet. "What happens then? Are you going to stay up here all by yourself?"

Mandy nodded. "That was the original plan."

"You sound like maybe that's not your intent anymore. Have your plans changed?"

She squinted out at the sunrise. "I'm not entirely sure," she told him. "I thought I knew what I wanted, but being here these past months... I'm not the same person I was when I came. I'm not really sure who I am anymore, but I'm not convinced I want to be up here all by myself, as you put it. If you'd asked me six months ago, I would've immediately replied that solitude was what I wanted, but now, after being up here with your dad all this time, I don't know if I could face it without his quiet presence. I'd miss him too much, you know?" She looked over at him, and there was a glistening of tears in her eyes.

Touched, he reached out and placed one hand on her shoulder, offering comfort. "There are other choices. You can go anywhere. Do anything. You don't have to stay here. If you want to stay with the park service, there are many other posts you could fill. And, if you want to do something different, there are a million opportunities out there." He wondered if he should keep going and then decided to throw caution to the wind. "I could even help you find something. I've got friends all over. If you don't want to stay here, what kind of place would you like to go?"

"Someplace safe," she replied immediately, then looked up at him, fear in her eyes. "I mean—"

"Don't backpedal," he told her quietly, moving closer and putting his arm around her shoulders. "I've figured out by now that something bad happened to you. Something you don't want to talk about. I respect that. Lord knows, I've had some bad stuff go down in my life and my career. I've been where you are. But I want you to know, you won't always be in the abyss. There is a way out. You'll find it. I can tell. You're a fighter. You won't give up, and you'll prevail over whatever it is that's trying to hold you down."

"How can you be so sure?" Her voice was the merest whisper.

She was so close. She looked so lost. All he had to do was move a few inches, and then...

He kissed her again. Tentatively, at first, in case she didn't want it. She surprised him by moving into his embrace and clinging to him. Her lips moved on his, and it was her that deepened the kiss, sliding her tongue into his mouth, making him stifle a groan.

Mandy was lost in Wil's kiss. Again. For a split second, she wondered if she was out of her ever-loving mind, then sensation took over, and she didn't think anymore. She could only feel. The solid warmth of his shoulders under her hands, the slight rasp of his cheeks against her skin. The wonder of his lips against hers. It was all just too much for her to process and still be able to think clearly.

Thinking, she decided, was overrated.

She reveled in his touch, leaning into his embrace when, for months, she'd flinched from every other form of human contact. She had thought she might never be able to bear a man touching her in even the most innocent of ways, but she'd been wrong. Ever since she'd met Wil, she hadn't minded casual contact—much less this kind of more intimate touching. She almost felt like her old self. The person she'd been before the incident. Almost.

Before too long, the kiss just wasn't enough. She wanted to touch his skin. More importantly, she wanted him to touch her. How long had it been since she'd been touched with care, respect and passion by a man?

After being kissed by Wil, she wasn't sure she'd ever had that trifecta of affection from any man in her past. Oh, they'd been nice enough, but the few men she'd allowed past first base, so to speak, hadn't had the enticing combination she felt when Wil kissed her.

Maybe she was imagining it, but she felt as if he truly cared, in some small way, and that he also respected her boundaries. He didn't push. He waited for her to increase the tempo, the pressure, the intimacy. He let her set the pace, for which she was so incredibly grateful. It was almost as if he knew what she'd been through, but nobody knew the full story. Not here. She'd left all that behind when she'd started over—as much as she could. The people around her might not know every detail of what had happened to her, but she carried it around with her like a dark cloud, just waiting to rain all over her new life given the least provocation.

Shoving that thought aside, Mandy decided to live for the moment...and this moment was delicious in every way. Turning more fully toward Wil, she practically climbed over him to straddle his thighs. The move took her a little off-balance, but Wil was there to support her back, holding her steady. It was a metaphor, really, for this entire thing. He was there, steadying her as she tried to push past the boundaries that had been imposed on her by life. By the terrible things that had once happened to her.

Wil might not realize it, but in that moment, she began to trust him. Really trust him. He didn't know about her past, but he was sensitive enough to realize something about her was a little different. Rather than steamroll over her—something he could easily do with his greater physical strength and incredible sex appeal—he was patient and kind...and sexy as hell.

She ran her hands over his shoulders and wanted to touch his skin. He was wearing his jacket open with a T-shirt under it. He didn't seem to feel the cold like she did. Of course, they were generating enough heat between them that the night air, and its colder temperature was really the last thing on her mind. All she could focus on was Wil and how badly she wanted to feel her skin against his.

She deepened the kiss as she ran her hands down over his chest and lower, along washboard abs that made her insides squirm with appreciation. He was rock hard all over. Big and muscular without looking like a hulk. His physique was that of someone who used his body for more than just lifting weights. He was a man of action, and his body reflected his active lifestyle. She'd been fitter than she was now at one time. Before the incident, she'd had an athlete's form, but the long recovery had limited her activities, and the psychological effects had been even more limiting.

As a result, her hard-won muscles had gone a bit flabbier than she liked. She'd been working hard at reviving her stamina and her muscle tone since coming here, but it was slow going. She wondered, self-consciously, if Wil would mind, but he hadn't known her before. He had no idea her current look was a new one for her, and she had no doubt that he was attracted to her. A man didn't kiss a woman the way he was kissing her without being more than a little interested in her.

She moved on his lap, daring greatly, sliding farther up on his thighs. She wanted to know if he was feeling this amazing attraction as much as she. She wanted to feel his maleness against her softest spots and know that he wanted her as much as she wanted him.

One big hand cupped her ass and squeezed. She moaned, loving the feel of his strong fingers against her. She squirmed a little closer, and he helped, rubbing his hand over her and encouraging her to move even closer…until, finally, she felt his erection against the seam of her crotch. Layers of fabric separated them, but nothing could hide the steel rod in his pants from the heated heart of her that had wanted to know the feel of him so badly.

His free hand went to the zip of her jacket and pulled the tab down slowly as he broke the kiss and looked deep into her eyes. She didn't stop him. She would never stop him. Not when she saw such desire and caring and tenderness in his eyes.

"I want to touch you," he whispered. "Will you let me touch you?"

Mutely, she nodded, and he unzipped her jacket completely, parting it. She was wearing a V-neck sleep shirt underneath, with no bra. She hadn't bothered to dress much before coming outside to join the guys on the porch. She'd only thrown on a pair of jeans, boots and her jacket.

Wil glanced down, his eyes widening as he saw the way her nipples poked at the thin fabric of the slinky shirt. She grinned at his reaction. That one look made her feel more secure, somehow. Secure in the knowledge that he desired her, even if she was a bit curvier than she had once been.

He ran one finger down along the edge of her V-neck shirt, stopping at the bottom of the V and pushing the fabric downward, as if testing how stretchy it was. Lucky for them both, it was very stretchy, indeed. He soon discovered that fact and ran his fingers under the edge, grasping it and pulling it downward, freeing her breasts.

Framed by the distorted neckline, she felt incredibly aroused to have him looking at and touching her breasts. He ran his thumbs over her distended nipples as he cupped her softness in his big hands. Then, he lowered his mouth and nuzzled them, driving her wild.

When his mouth opened over one and sucked it inside, she shivered and suppressed a moan as best she could. She hadn't been touched this way in so very long. Actually, she wasn't sure she'd ever been touched quite like this, with this reverence...this respect...this incredibly masterful touch that drove her passions right into the stratosphere.

Only Wil had ever affected her so quickly and so well. He moved his attention to the other side, his agile tongue sweeping circles around the nub that peaked for his efforts. Mandy threw her head back and strained forward, into his mouth, wanting more. So much more...

Just then, the howl of a wolf penetrated the fog of desire. It was close. Alarmingly close. Mandy stilled, unsure of what to do, her mind in a bit of a stupor.

CHAPTER ELEVEN

Wil lifted his head and shook it once, then twice, trying to break free of the sensual spell that had almost consumed him. Touching Mandy was like a drug to his senses, but he couldn't afford to be distracted. Not when there was danger nearby.

Though it was one of the hardest things he'd ever had to do, Wil drew back, setting Mandy away from him. He met her gaze, seeing the dazed look in her eyes that he'd put there. A momentary surge of masculine pride hit him, but he knew he couldn't afford to bask in such foolishness. The wolves wouldn't come this close unless there was a problem. He helped her right her clothing and buttoned her up a bit.

"You'd better go inside. The wildlife is

getting restless." He tried to make it sound like a joke, but his voice was raspy. He wanted nothing more than to continue what they'd been doing to its likely, highly pleasurable conclusion, but he dare not. Not right now, at any rate.

He stood and took her with him. Leaving her little choice, he hustled her back to her trailer and left her with a quick kiss on the steps before she disappeared inside. He knew her head was probably still reeling from the quick change of plans, but it couldn't be helped.

Instead of going back to the porch, Wil headed toward where he'd heard the wolf's howl. He wasn't surprised to find Liam waiting just inside the tree line for him.

"Sorry for the interruption, but there's news," Liam said quickly, in a low voice.

A giant wolf was just behind him, and Wil now knew that behemoth of a canine was a shifter. He nodded at the furry monster to acknowledge the wolf's participation.

"Those foreign fellows are definitely hunters, and they're hunting you, Wil. And Rick. They've been flashing photos of you two all over these mountains. Luckily, the few locals know enough not to give out any information, even if they'd seen you, but the hikers and day trippers are another story. The hunters are on this mountain. Our wolf friends are leading them astray, but I'm not sure how long they can keep the hunters entertained and confused. How is your dad for travel?" Liam asked.

"I think he's good to go, though we should

check with Rick to be absolutely sure," Wil replied. "Do we need to bug out now?"

"No, I think you should be good for another few hours. Even the hunters have to sleep, and they've been run ragged all night. They made camp, and the Alpha here, has some people watching them. Just pack up and be ready. I'll call my dad again and see what he's come up with. He was going to call in a few favors, so our evac might be…uh…somewhat non-traditional." Liam's smile was cunning and made Wil wonder exactly what kind of *non-traditional* help Lester Kinkaid had at his disposal, but he supposed he'd find out soon enough. "Just be ready to go wheels up when our ride gets here."

"Will do," Wil replied, then looked at the wolf. "Thank you for your assistance, Alpha," Wil added. It never hurt to be polite. The wolf nodded in reply.

As Wil walked out of the trees a few minutes later, the sun was hiding behind clouds. He knew, with that innate sense that had come with his new gift, that it would rain later. Unless he did something about it. Right now, he'd wait and see what the day called for. He was loath to interfere with the natural rhythms of the weather unless he had a good reason to do so. For now, he'd let the clouds build. They might come in handy later.

Rick was waiting for Wil on the porch as he approached the cabin. They went indoors to discuss Liam's intel while preparing breakfast. Senior joined them at the table, and when he heard what was likely to happen, he started making plans to leave with them later that day.

"Where's Mandy?" Wil asked, when they were finishing breakfast. "Doesn't she eat with you?"

"Not all the time," Senior admitted. "Some days, she goes out early on patrol. There's that eagle pair she's keeping an eye on. She might've gone out early to check on them."

"Dad, I don't want her alone on this mountain when the enemy gets here looking for us." Wil's heart dropped as he considered what might happen to her when the hunters arrived to find their quarry had flown the coop.

"I could ask her to go down the mountain to the main ranger station, I guess," Senior said, scratching his head. "I'd already planned to ask the wolves to keep an eye on her after I leave. It doesn't sit right, leaving her all alone up here."

"I know what you mean. With the enemy closing in, it feels a little too much like leaving her holding the bag," Rick said, unexpectedly. "I think we should take her with us. We can always return her later, after the threat passes."

Wil was relieved to hear his friend and partner on this mission wouldn't fight him on this. Wil had already decided that, somehow, he needed to get Mandy off this mountain—at least until after the danger passed. How they were going to manage that was another question.

"Thing is," Wil broached the topic he'd been mulling over silently, "how much can we really tell her? We have to get her to agree to leave with us. We can't kidnap the woman."

"Leave it to me," Senior said confidently. "I'll say we're going somewhere so I can try an experimental treatment, and I'd like her to come along for moral support. She's kind-hearted enough that she wouldn't leave me in the lurch if I grovel." Senior chuckled at his own word.

"Okay, but what happens when we get where we're going and it's not a hospital?" Wil asked his dad.

"One step at a time, son."

At that moment, the howling started up outside the cabin, and all three men rose to their feet. Rick and Wil produced firearms that never strayed far from their sides...and so did Senior. More significantly, Senior pulled his favorite sniper rifle from under the kitchen counter, where he'd somehow had it stashed out of sight, and headed for the window at the front of the cabin.

Wil saw in a moment that his father had covertly set up a sniper's nest to the side of the window. He had a low stool that was on wheels located in just the right spot. Even as Wil watched, shaking his head in wonderment, his dad pulled out an improvised ghillie suit top that he'd had secreted beneath the stool. Throwing it over his head, he was as camouflaged as he could be. As he opened the window, he looked at his son. The look on his face spoke clearer than words.

The raised eyebrow said it all. Wil could

almost hear his dad's voice in his mind saying, "Well, what are you waiting for?"

Spurred into action, Wil followed Rick out the door, melting into the shadows of the porch.

After the initial alarm, the wolves that Wil knew were slinking around the perimeter of the property had gone unnaturally silent. When the first shot rang out, it was a catalyst for hell to rain down on the small cabin at the top of a mountain. Chaos reigned as the boom of handguns vied with the growls of animals and the screams of their victims.

Wil and Rick were engaged at the side of the cabin, using Mandy's trailer for cover while Senior took carefully placed shots with his trusty rifle from the cabin's open window. There were a lot more assailants than Wil had expected. It sounded as if the enemy had brought a small army up to the top of the mountain, and if not for the shifters taking them on with teeth and claws, the three human men would have been woefully outnumbered.

The shifters were almost herding the enemy into the open, pushing them into the clearing in front of the cabin with their continuing attacks. Wil recognized the Alpha wolf he'd seen with Liam. He saw that wolf take three shots to the chest and just keep on moving forward, as if nothing had happened. After this was all over, Wil was going to have to have a serious talk with Liam. These shifters were amazing in action.

Then, a massive roar sounded, and a giant

lion—which had to be Liam, in the fur, so to speak—pounced on the guy who was still shooting at the Alpha wolf. Liam's massive jaws closed on the man's neck, and Wil heard the audible crunch as the enemy went down under Liam's claws and teeth, never to rise again. The wolves all around were launching similar attacks, working in teams, to take down the enemy who didn't seem surprised by the Pack's attack.

That, right there, told Wil that these enemy soldiers knew a lot more about the supernatural world than most people. It also made them fair game. Especially since they seemed to have no qualms about shooting anyone and anything that moved. Decision made, Wil was about to call the lightning to help clear the area when Mandy entered the clearing nearby. She had come running and was armed with a very neat 9mm handgun that Wil had not expected.

What surprised him even more was that she took cover behind a tree stump and started firing at the men who were still firing at the cabin. Between Mandy's handgun, Senior's sniper rifle, the animals, and Rick and Wil's continued barrage, the enemy numbers dwindled significantly. Many of them fell to the wolf Pack, augmented by one seriously badass lion shifter. Others fell to gunfire. Still others fell back, retreating into the woods with shifters hot on their trails. They wouldn't get far.

Within moments of its start, the firefight was over. Potentially. Wil looked over at Mandy and realized he had a lot of explaining to do. She'd seen the animals fighting on their side. And she'd probably seen Senior shooting steady, without a sign of the tremor that had affected his hands when Wil and Rick had arrived.

She looked a little shell shocked, though, and his first instinct was to offer comfort. Signaling to Rick to cover his move, he ran, crouching to make himself a smaller target, to the large tree stump she had hidden behind while making her shots count. He put his back to hers and covered her back while she kept watch on the front.

"Is it over?" she whispered.

"Almost," Wil declared. "If you want to get to the cabin, we'll cover you."

"I would, but I'm not sure my legs are steady enough, right now. It's been a while since I've been in a shootout," she shocked him by saying.

"You are just full of surprises, aren't you?" he mused, a grin splitting his lips.

"I was a cop in Seattle," she revealed.

He wasn't surprised after witnessing her response to the crisis, just now. She had good instincts and was cool when it counted. He was impressed all over again. She was hell on wheels, and he'd be damned if that wasn't a weird sort of turn on for him.

"Like I said, full of surprises," he replied, shaking his head as he smiled.

"I have a few questions."

Oh, boy. Here it comes, he thought. "I just bet you do," he muttered in reply.

"First, who the heck is shooting at us and

why? And, after that, can anyone explain why there's a freaking *lion* running loose in the middle of Glacier National Park?" Her voice rose in disbelief, and Wil knew the cat—or lion, as it were—was definitely out of the bag. "And what's up with the wolves? I know your dad is friendly with one of them, but I've never seen a wolf pack fight alongside a bunch of people, much less a *lion*. This is some weird shit."

The fact that she'd cussed for the first time in his hearing told him that she was more than a little upset, but she was holding it together, keeping her eyes on the tree line, her head on a swivel, as his was, watching for the enemy. She was vigilant, even though the shooting had stopped.

"Let's get you to the cabin, and we can talk there. You're right. There is a lot of weird shit happening right now, and you deserve to know about some of it, at least." He sighed. "How are your legs? Think you can make a run for the porch?"

"Trailer first," she corrected him. "Let's retrace your route here, see how I do, then go from there."

"All right," he agreed readily. "Countdown from three when you're ready to go. I'll cover and follow." He made a series of hand signals for Rick and his dad to read, explaining what they were planning to do.

The move back to the cabin proceeded in stages and didn't take long. Mandy was steadier than she'd thought, and it took only a minute or so before they were inside the cabin, in relative safety. Rick followed them in once they saw Liam in the woods, signaling that the wolf Pack would keep watch on the perimeter.

Wil was trying to formulate some way of explaining the lion's presence when Mandy saw his dad, and her attention shifted to the way Senior was walking around without assistance, spry as he'd been before the illness that had affected him so badly. She went right up to Senior and shook her head, her mouth open in wonder.

"William, what exactly is going on here? You were a million years old just the other day, and now, you look better than I've ever seen you." Her gaze shifted around the room, lighting on Wil. "Somebody has a lot of explaining to do. Not that I'm not thrilled to see you looking so good," she hastened to add, turning back to Wil's dad with a smile. "Does this mean you're no longer at death's door?"

Senior smiled back at her. "Nowhere near that particular door, at the moment. Not for a good many years, according to Dr. Rick over there. He's worked a little magic."

Wil couldn't help but think that explanation wasn't too far from the truth, yet it told her nothing of the substance of what had happened. He had to hand it to his dad. The old man wrote the book on vague explanations and obfuscation.

CHAPTER TWELVE

Mandy couldn't believe the changes in William. He was so much better. He was able to stand and walk properly without shuffling or grabbing onto the nearest piece of furniture for support. He even looked younger without the lines of pain that had seemed permanently etched into his face. He looked like the photos she'd seen of him that had been taken before the illness had ravaged him so badly.

Just then, a phone beeped, and Rick reached into his vest pocket and pulled out what looked like a satellite phone. He turned away, murmuring low into the handset as he answered the call.

"Which one of you wants to explain about the lion?" Mandy raised her eyebrow and looked between father and son, waiting to hear what kind of possible explanation there could be for the weird behavior of those animals outside.

"Have you ever heard of shapeshifters?" Wil asked, making a pained face.

"Sure. Old Indian legends talk about people who turn into animals and vice versa," she replied at once. She'd learned a lot about Native American legends since moving to Montana. "You can't seriously expect me to believe…"

"They're real," Wil replied quickly. "I know, it's crazy, but it's real. Honest. I only learned about them recently myself, but I've been working alongside them for a while, and they're just like normal people, only with much sharper senses, and they can turn, at will, into their animal."

"This is all supposed to be Top Secret," Senior put in, a frown deepening the lines on his face. "I don't know what they're going to think about you finding out, Mandy." He scratched his head, still frowning. "There could be repercussions."

Wil didn't like the sound of that. "I think you'd better come with us," he said to Mandy.

"Come with you? Where?" Mandy appeared both surprised and alarmed.

"I'm not sure yet. We're supposed to be getting emergency transport, but I'm not sure what the initial destination is. Ultimately, we're going back east, to where we're stationed, and Dad's decided to come with us. At least until we figure out his next step."

"You're leaving?" Mandy looked stricken as she gazed over at Wil's dad.

Senior walked over to her and put one hand on her shoulder. His pace was steady, his gait balanced, his motions silent. He was nearly back to his old self, Wil was glad to see.

"You know I can't stay here like this," Senior explained in a soft voice. "There would be too many questions."

"I can see that, but..." Mandy looked so lost, Wil wanted to put his arms around her. Apparently, his dad thought the same, offering Mandy a fatherly hug. "I'm going to miss you, William." Mandy hugged Senior, and Wil could see the genuine affection between the two of them.

Mandy was one in a million. She'd been prepared to see Wil's dad—a complete stranger when this all started—through his final days. Mandy had a big heart to dedicate herself to such a course.

"Come with us, Mandy. At least for a couple of days. Until things settle down and I'm certain you'll be safe here," Senior coaxed. "There could be more of them, after all, and I can't stomach the idea of leaving you here to possibly face them alone."

Rick turned back to them, ending his call. "Kinkaid called in a favor and is routing us through a merc company he knows out of Wyoming. They're sending a chopper with an ETA of twenty minutes. They'll call with updates as they get closer."

A low whistle sounded from the doorway

before anyone could answer. Liam was standing in the open door, back in uniform. The damn cat moved so silently, he'd had to draw their attention to his presence with that whistle.

"The Pack is guarding the perimeter. They're also going to take care of clean up," Liam told them. "They'll make things right with the park service, too. Turns out, most of the other rangers are friends of theirs, if you know what I mean," Liam winked, smiling a bit. "And Colonel Owens, sir, I have Commander Kinkaid on the line for you." Liam held out a sat phone toward Wil's dad.

Senior took the phone and went toward the back of the cabin, opening the armory. If they only had twenty minutes, he was probably going to pack some more of his collection to take with him.

"What do you say, Mandy?" Wil asked her quietly, going closer to stand next to her. "I'd like for you to come with us." He held out his hand, praying she'd take it.

She placed her hand in his, and he found he could breathe again.

"Should I pack an overnight bag?" she asked, uncertainty in her eyes.

Wil nodded. "I'll go with you, just in case."

She nodded, and they headed out of the cabin and over to the trailer. She packed while he stood by the door. She grabbed a knapsack and began throwing clothes into it. She wasn't a neat packer, which amused him for some reason.

"Is it okay to bring my weapons?" she asked,

reminding him again that she was no helpless flower, but a former police officer with experience in *gunfights*, as she'd called them.

"Sure. Where do you think my dad went? I have no doubt he's packing his favorite rifles at this very moment." Wil let his amusement sound in his voice.

Mandy surprised him yet again by going over to a wall near the bed and opening a hidden compartment. Inside was a nice collection of handguns. Everything from a .38 Special to a 9mm Ruger. He noted how she handled each piece with precision and skill, making sure everything was unloaded before stowing them in a carrying case she had to have had specially made for her collection. Everything had a padded slot, and the case locked with a combination. Nice.

The case went into the big knapsack, and then, the whole thing was slung over her shoulder. She had put the gun she'd been using back into the shoulder holster she'd been wearing under her jacket. She exchanged her Park Service jacket for an unmarked one and was ready to go.

Wil escorted her back to the cabin. He would have taken more time, but he felt the pressure they were under. He'd feel a whole lot easier about this situation once they were off this mountain. He couldn't help but feel that they weren't out of the woods yet—literally or figuratively.

When they arrived back at the cabin, his father had finished his phone call and had a large rifle case at his feet, along with a rucksack holding some clothes. He was ready to go. Rick had done Wil a favor and grabbed his pack from the room they'd been sharing and had that ready near the door, as well.

"Lester is going to send someone out to take over here and clear things with Chief Buchanon," Senior told Mandy and Wil. "Apparently, he knows Buchanon from way back," Senior rolled his eyes. "These shifters are very good at hiding their presence. I had no idea so many of my colleagues, both here and in the Army, were like that." Senior shook his head. "At any rate. Les will arrange for his guy to pack up the rest of the house and send it on to us wherever we end up, depending on how things play out. For now, everything we leave behind will be kept secure, so no need to worry on that score."

"Sounds good, Dad," Wil said, into the silence.

Rick's satellite phone dinged, and he looked at the screen then up again. "Evac is almost here. We should go out to meet them. Chopper will land in the clearing in front of the house, but they don't want to stay on the ground long."

"Can't blame them," Senior muttered and hefted his own bags, leading the way out the door of the only home he'd known for the past few decades. He didn't look back, and Wil tried to achieve the same stoicism.

They all took up positions just off the porch, keeping to the shadows as much as possible.

Everybody was on guard, and the forest seemed to be holding its breath.

Wil felt the preternatural silence of the woods and realized something was wrong. He sent out a little gust of wind, seeking answers, but it hadn't even gone ten yards when he felt a wave of what could only be magic knock him flat on his ass.

He looked around and realized it had knocked everyone else down, too. Even Liam. And, what was worse, he couldn't move. He was pinned to the ground.

If this…whatever it was…had pinned Liam, it had likely pinned down all of the wolves as well. Shit! There definitely were more of the enemy, and these were armed with the kind of weapons Wil didn't really know how to counter. Not yet, anyway. He'd have to think on his feet—or flat on his back, as the case may be.

Wil looked up at the sky and wondered if he could still affect the weather, even though he couldn't even move his toes, much less his fingers. Always before, he'd made some gesture with his hand or fingers to guide the energy where he wanted it to go, but he would have to figure another way this time. Lives hung in the balance. Not just his, or his colleagues', or his dad's, but Mandy's life. And her life was suddenly more important to him than any other.

As he was thinking all this, five people walked into the clearing in front of the house. Calmly, but with purpose, they walked into view and spread out, taking up positions equidistant from each other. They were chanting. These, then, were the bastards who were doing the magic that had everybody pinned in place.

Wil knew what to do.

He called the clouds. And then, he called the lightning...

The sky roiled at his command, churning violently. It was working. He could feel the energy building. When it was just right, he loosed the power, directing it with his will, exactly where he wanted it to go.

Five bolts of fiery destruction rained down on the five people who were chanting. The sharp smell of ozone filled the air, and the crash of thunder coincided with the Wil's ability to move once again. He sat upright, looking around as his ears rang with white noise. His hearing would take time to recover from the incredible booms and cracks of thunder so very close to them.

The five people who had been chanting were all dead, hit by lightning at point-blank range. As far as he could see, there were no other imminent threats, but Wil remembered the helicopter that was coming for them. It couldn't land in the weather he'd called. Quickly, he looked up at the sky and sent a zephyr of wind to do his bidding, clearing the clouds and sending them off again with his thanks.

Rick was shaking his head as Liam rose to his feet and prowled the area. Wil checked on his dad while Mandy looked around, clearly bewildered.

"What the hell was that?" she shouted, clearly unable to moderate her volume with the ringing in her ears.

Wil shook his head. "It's a long story," he replied finally.

"Chopper will be here in five," Rick reported. He was standing now, looking down at his phone. "They'd like a bit more clearance, and a little less wind, if you can manage it."

Wil nodded and pointed at the sky with one finger. Immediately, the hole in the clouds became wider. Mandy looked from Wil, to his pointing finger, to the sky and back again, her mouth dropping open. The clouds blew away as quickly as they had come, and the sun reappeared.

"No freaking way," she murmured loud enough for him to hear, which brought a rueful smile to his lips.

"Wind is going now," Wil reported to Rick, all the while holding Mandy's wide gaze. "Tell them they can land at their discretion." He would have a lot of explaining to do, he knew, but in his heart, it was a relief to have her see a bit of what he could do.

"That's some freaky new ability you have there, son," Senior said as he climbed slowly to his feet. Mandy rushed to assist. "You greased them all in a split second." Senior looked over at the dead enemies and nodded, his face solemn. "I would've liked to know what they thought they were doing up here, but I suspect there would have been no way to neutralize them without killing them. You did the right thing."

Wil was touched by his father's approval. He'd never really had to answer to anyone other than his commanding officer for his decisions out in the field. He discovered it felt good to know his dad—an experienced warrior of legendary proportions—approved of Wil's actions.

"That he did," Liam agreed, reappearing suddenly. "There's often no other way to deal with dark magic than to smite it where it stands." Liam offered Wil his hand, a grin on his face. "And you've got that smiting thing down pat, friend."

Wil chuckled, returning the shifter's handshake. "Sorry about the noise."

Liam barked a laugh as he stepped back. "Those five had everyone in the woods down flat on the ground, too," he reported. "They all came free when you broke the spell with the lightning strike. Our ears are all ringing, but that's a small price to pay for taking out five enemy magic users in one fell swoop. You done good, Thor."

Wil shook his head and groaned. He'd been fighting against that nickname for a while, but after today, he suspected he'd lost that particular battle.

"Are the wolves okay?" Senior asked Liam, moving closer.

"They're fine, sir. They're back on patrol, and so far, these five stragglers are the only ones. Thing is, the wolves didn't see them."

Liam scratched the back of his neck, his expression clearly troubled. "These mages were able to hide their presence and walk straight through almost the entire wolf Pack to attack us here. That speaks of black magic, which is one of the worst forms of dark power. The Alpha is going to call our leadership and make a report. Chances are, they'll send out an investigator so we can get more intel about these five and where they might have come from."

Senior nodded. "I'm glad someone will be looking into this. It doesn't sit right, being attacked on this mountain. I always thought nothing could ever touch me here, but it seems I was badly mistaken."

He might have said more, but at that moment, the helicopter made its appearance, swooping in from the tree line and landing with a roar of its blades. It was a larger model that had to be military surplus. It set down, and a squad of armed men in camo fatigues piled out and set up a perimeter. One separated from the group and jogged up to Liam.

They exchanged a few words nobody else could hear over the roar of the chopper blades, and then, Liam gave the signal for everybody to load onto the helicopter. Rick and Mandy were helping Senior, who was recovering more slowly from the effect of the magic and thunder than the younger folks. Liam was still talking with the newcomer, which meant Wil was on point. He moved ahead to the chopper and checked things out. Only the pilots were aboard, sitting way up front in the cockpit. The entire cargo area was available for them, with fold-out seats along the side walls.

Wil turned to help his dad, if necessary, but Senior was looking better with each step. He mounted the ramp into the chopper and took a seat on one side, Rick settling in beside him. Wil took their baggage and stowed it nearby, keeping an eye on balancing the load, having been transported on enough helicopters to know that sometimes they could be a little sensitive to weight variances.

He caught Mandy's eye and pointed to the seat on the opposite wall from his dad's for her. She nodded and stowed her own bag under her seat, securing it with a bungee to the seat frame. He put his own bags near the seat next to her then went back to the ramp to check on Liam's progress.

CHAPTER THIRTEEN

Liam and the other man came up the ramp together, then the new guy hit the button to retract the ramp and seal the compartment. After which, he gave the pilots the signal, and they were airborne. Wil was surprised he'd left his people behind, but in another way, he was glad somebody with some firepower would be there to help the wolf Pack, in case more trouble started on the mountain after Wil and his party left. He didn't like leaving the wolves who'd been so good to his dad in the lurch.

Wil was seated next to Liam along one side wall of the chopper, while the other man sat next to Senior. Liam leaned in to make himself heard over the noise of the spinning blades.

"That's Major Moore," Liam said, indicating the man who had come in on the chopper. "He left a squad of his people behind to secure the area, and he'll liaise with the shifter hierarchy and my dad. They're old friends."

"Who's his CO?" Wil asked, a bit confused by the way Liam referred to the new man. Was he legit military? If not, why was Liam giving him the rank of Major?

"Nobody, now, though his group has been known to work missions for Admiral Morrow on occasion. Major Moore retired from the Army several years ago and formed a specialized mercenary group known in shifter circles as the Wraiths. All of his guys are ex-Special Forces and shifters, as well. They're on the right side of the battle between good and evil." Liam looked at Moore, who was speaking with Wil's dad as if they were old buddies. "You know, when the major heard your dad was involved, he decided to fly out with the squad. Seems he and your father go way back."

"Seriously?" Wil asked, taking a fresh look at the way the men across the way were interacting. They certainly looked as if they were reminiscing. Both were grinning and seemed easy in each other's company.

"Moore doesn't look it, but he's probably quite a bit older than your dad. We don't show our ages the way you guys do. We hit prime and stay there for a few centuries, if we're lucky," Liam clarified.

Wil looked at Liam sharply. "Centuries?" Wil had realized shifters lived longer than regular people, but he hadn't quite appreciated how much longer. The idea of these people living for hundreds of years blew Wil's mind.

Liam shrugged. "If we don't get killed in battle or some other way. It's the magic, you know? It's just the way we're made." He said that as if it was no big deal, but Wil was impressed. "We're headed for Wyoming. That's where the Wraiths are headquartered. Major Moore said he's still working on coordinating transport from there back to our base, but it should be sorted out shortly. In the meantime, we're welcome on his mountain, but I wanted you to understand the setup they have. The major's the Alpha of the mercenary company, and his brother is the Alpha of a large wolf Pack that lives on and around the mountain. We'll be their guests, and we're lucky that your dad already seems to understand wolves, but you, Rick and especially Mandy are going to have to adapt. If you need help with shifter etiquette, I'm your man. Better to ask me than to make a blunder that gets the whole Pack up in arms, all right?"

"Got it," Wil replied, almost, but not quite, insulted that Liam expected him to need guidance on how to be polite.

Still, shifter culture was still a new concept to Wil, and he suspected there were very different codes of conduct among them. At least Liam was offering to act as a guide, of sorts, to prevent any misunderstandings. Wil knew Liam didn't have to do that, and he appreciated the gesture.

Mandy's mind was working overtime trying

to come to terms with everything that had just happened. She'd barely had a chance to catch her breath, and now, she was flying in what looked like a military helicopter, though it had none of the official markings she would have expected. So, it was a *privately owned* military helo? Did these people have their own private army? And, if so, was there a battle going on that the rest of the world seemed to not know about at all?

She was very much afraid that was exactly the case. She watched the men talk but didn't participate. The noise from the blades of the helo were just too loud. And, honestly, she felt a bit shell-shocked after all that had just taken place. Better to sit quietly and try to regain some sort of equilibrium.

As it was, she had only a vague notion of where they were going. A mountain in Wyoming, she'd been told. Great. There were *a lot* of mountains in Wyoming. Which particular mountain they would be landing on remained a mystery.

When they began to descend, she felt the change in air pressure in her ears. She'd always been sensitive to altitude and pressure changes that way. A few minutes later, she felt the chopper jolt a bit when it touched the ground and then finally settled as the blades began their long spin-down.

The men rose, and the man who had come in with the enormous helicopter lowered the ramp. William touched her arm, getting her attention as the noise level lowered and she was able to hear herself think again.

"You okay, sweetheart?" William asked, his old eyes filled with kindness. He was such a good man. His son was proving to be a lot like him.

"I'll be okay," she replied. She wasn't sure how it was all going to work out, but she had learned to keep a positive attitude over the past months.

"Stick with either myself or my boy, and you'll be fine." He patted her arm twice then removed his hand. He was so much stronger than he had been. She marveled at the change in him as she watched him walk down the ramp next to the mission commander.

Mandy had never been in the military, but she recognized the manner and stance of the men all around her as she walked down the ramp into the late afternoon sun. They were either current or retired military. Of that, she had little doubt.

It was fractionally warmer here, a little farther south as the chopper flew. The sun was shining, and the men were in earnest discussion just a few steps ahead of her. Only when she caught sight of the woman waiting for them on the wooded path that led away from the helipad's clearing did Mandy think about how outnumbered by men she'd been this whole time.

She'd gotten used to being one of the few female officers in her department, but it had been a while since she'd been in that sort of situation. She'd been a civilian—well, a ranger—for a while now, and the civilian world was a lot more diverse gender-wise than her former profession.

The men stopped when they reached the woman who waited just under the cover of the trees, and the man who'd been on the helicopter stepped over to her and put his arm around her waist. He made the introductions while Mandy paused to listen along with the others.

"Everybody, this is my mate, Maria." He turned a loving look on the woman and spoke directly to her. "Maybe you could take charge of Ranger Clarke and help her get settled in the guest cabin while I show the men the barracks?"

Smiling, Maria broke away from her mate and walked up to Mandy. "Is that all right with you, Ranger Clarke? I'm sure once you all have a chance to catch your breath, there'll be some big debriefing, but you'll probably want to see where you'll be sleeping first, right?"

Mandy looked at Wil, receiving a reassuring nod. She was in these people's hands, for better or worse, and Maria seemed like a nice woman. Mandy certainly didn't sense any threat from her. Not like the military men all around. Maria was most definitely a civilian. Mandy found that reassuring.

"That sounds good, Maria. Call me Mandy," she replied, trying to sound casual, when in reality, she wanted a few precious minutes alone in a quiet place to try to gather her spinning thoughts.

Maria's smile brightened further. "Great. Follow me."

The guest cabin appeared both rustic and charming as they approached. Maria was chatty enough to set Mandy more at ease. She gave Mandy a little tour of the area as they walked and indicated that the smaller structure she'd be using was situated next to the so-called barracks that would serve for the men tonight.

"Most of the regular guys have their own cabins all over the mountain," Maria said. "And I have a rehab center closer to the road that connects us with civilization, but I bring the more serious cases up here and treat them in that barn over there." Maria pointed toward a giant barn just visible through the trees. "I'm a veterinarian," she clarified. "I treat mostly wild animals that need rehab before being reintroduced into the wild, but I do get the occasional exotic or domestic down at the clinic."

Mandy was intrigued. "What sorts of animals are in the barn?"

"Currently, I have a juvenile black bear, a senior bobcat and a cougar that all need a bit more time here before they can go back out on their own. Then, there's a young eagle who flew into some barbed wire and got stuck." She shook her head. "Poor thing. I get a lot of raptors this time of year for some reason," she went on as they neared the cabin. "If you're interested, I can give you a tour of the barn later. We make them as comfortable as possible, so they all have big areas to themselves. We're lucky that we don't have to put them in small cages, but that also means that I have to warn newcomers not to go into the barn unless I've shown them how it's all set up first. Of course, the shifters are fine with wild animals, but you and I might have a problem if we ended up in the cougar's area without realizing it. Even half-healed, he still likes to pounce," Maria said with a toothy grin.

Maria left Mandy to get settled, and Mandy gratefully sat in the room's single easy chair, placed by the front window. She just needed a few minutes to catch her breath and figure out what in the world had happened today.

The next thing Mandy knew, there was a loud knocking on the cabin door as she roused from a totally unplanned nap in the easy chair. The action of the day must have taken more out of her than she realized because a quick glance out the window told her it was nearing dusk. She stood and shook off the last of the sleep that had snuck up on her and went to the door.

"Who is it?" she called out as she neared the wooden door.

"It's Wil. Are you okay?" He sounded concerned, and she opened the door to find him frowning.

"I'm fine. I just took an unscheduled nap." She still couldn't quite believe she'd fallen asleep, but stress had that effect sometimes.

Relief shone on his face. "When you didn't show for the debrief, I wondered, but Maria said to let you rest. They're getting ready to serve dinner now, so I figured I'd better come check on you."

Suddenly, her stomach rumbled, and she realized she hadn't eaten much today with everything that had happened. She rubbed her abdomen and stifled a yawn.

"Good call," she told Wil, shooting him a rueful glance. "Let me put my boots on, and you can show me where the food is. I'm afraid I don't really know my way around, except to stay out of the barn where Maria keeps the wild animals."

"Wild animals?" Wil looked surprised as Mandy went to fetch the boots she had kicked off before collapsing in the easy chair earlier.

"She's a veterinarian. Didn't they tell you? She rehabs wild animals, and they're kept in that barn. They're not in actual cages, so don't go in there unless she shows you how it's set up, she said."

Wil looked intrigued. "Nobody mentioned it," he replied.

"Maria said the shifters don't have any problem with the animals, but regular people need to be wary," she added as she slipped on her boots.

"That's probably why nobody thought to mention it. Dad, Rick and I have been holed up with Liam and Major Moore, plus a few of his men since we got here. They're all shifters here," Wil said in a low voice.

"Except for Maria, I think," Mandy said thoughtfully. "She may be with Major Moore, but I don't think she's one of them." Mandy still couldn't really believe they were having this conversation, talking about magical creatures as if they were commonplace.

"Look, Mandy, about what you saw before..." Wil ran one hand through his short hair, wincing as he seemed to search for words.

"You mean the way you crooked your little finger and moved an entire storm system out of the way so the helicopter could land? Or maybe the lightning that came out of nowhere to hit those five people—and only those five people—then fizzle away at your command? That was you, wasn't it? Or is my imagination even wilder than I thought?" She sounded a little hysterical, but she still couldn't quite believe what she'd seen.

Wil sighed and came closer. He reached out to her, touching her shoulders lightly with both of his hands. His gaze met hers, and his expression was very serious.

"It was me," he told her in a quiet voice. "Since an incident overseas, I can..." He faltered then tried again. "I can control the weather." He shook his head and let go of her shoulders, turning half away from her. "I know it sounds ridiculous."

"If I hadn't seen it myself, I'd think you were bonkers," she agreed.

He turned back, meeting her gaze with a flicker of hope in his own expression.

"It's crazy, right?" he said, chuckling wryly. "I mean, it's like something out of a comic book."

A thought occurred to her. "This somehow has something to do with why your father is suddenly so much better?"

Wil cringed a bit. "Not so much me, as Rick. He got...changed...a little, too. We've been in the same unit together for a few years, and he really does have a medical degree. He's our bioweapons specialist and medic, but when we encountered something magical in the ancient city of Babylon, suddenly Rick could heal without the use of medicine. That's how the rest of us knew that something truly amazing had happened to us all."

"All of you?" she asked, and he shook his head, looking torn.

"This is all strictly Top Secret, but since you saw what you saw..." Wil trailed off, turning toward the window and gazing out, his expression troubled. "I'm not supposed to tell you much—or anything, really—but I think you have a right to know. My dad isn't going to die, now. At least, not anytime soon. Not from illness. Rick took care of that, and he'll continue to keep an eye on Dad while we're traveling. I'm not sure where Dad's going to end up, but I think you can see that he can't go back to the mountain. Not without a whole lot of uncomfortable questions."

She nodded. "That makes sense."

"I think you'll have to come with us, back to base," he said, turning to face her again. "I'm sorry for disrupting your life, but my commanding officer will want to talk to you, and honestly, I want to be certain you're absolutely safe. There is a history with the people who have been hunting us. They like to use our friends and family against us." His expression turned grim.

"I'm not family," she protested without thinking. Only as she said it, did Mandy realize how much she'd like to be a part of Wil's family. To have William as a dad and Wil as a... A husband? A lover? The idea sent a ripple of awareness through her body.

CHAPTER FOURTEEN

"At the very least, you're a close friend of the family. Not many people would commit to seeing a dying man through his last days," Wil countered. He moved a step closer. "And I consider you a personal friend, and possibly more." He paused, shaking his head. "But you've seen the craziness in my life, right now. I'm not sure I can, in good conscience, subject anybody to that deliberately. As it is, I'm really sorry you got dragged into my drama as much as you have."

"It's okay," she told him in a quiet voice. It really was okay with her, she realized. She'd learned more about the hidden world in twenty-four hours than she'd ever have imagined, and she didn't want to go back to her plain existence where magic didn't live.

The healing of Wil's father was a miracle. A joyous miracle that proved to her that magic could do wondrous things. Sure, there might be a dark side to it, but that was true of all sources of power. She didn't, for one minute, think that Wil would ever use his abilities for bad purposes. He was a good person, through and through. Of that, she had not one doubt.

Slipping her boots on, she straightened and sent him a smile. "You said something about dinner?"

"Yeah," he agreed, shaking his head. "Right this way."

The rest would keep, for now, Mandy decided. She had to think things through before she could discuss this any further. She'd been given a lot of information in a short time. It would take some time to process it all.

Wil led her down one of these paths, and they came out at the entrance of a large welcoming sort of building that was clearly designed for group gatherings. It had large windows, through which she could see tables and chairs and people milling around a buffet table that ran the length of one wall. She realized there were many structures hidden among the trees, connected by winding pathways that couldn't be seen from above, considering the in-tact canopy of leaves and pine boughs overhead.

They went inside, and Wil seated Mandy next to Maria at a large dinner table, which was one of many spread around a large room. Maria was sitting next to the man from the helicopter,

Major Moore, and next to him was William, looking healthier than Mandy had ever seen him. William was deep in conversation with Moore as Wil took the seat beside Mandy around the circular table. Rick took the chair next to Wil, and Liam sat next to Rick. Next to William was a man introduced simply as Seth, whom she hadn't met before.

"How are you feeling?" Maria asked Mandy quietly as she settled into place beside her.

"Good, thanks. I didn't realize how tiring it all was, and I fell asleep in that pretty chair by the window," Mandy explained.

"I know. I went to fetch you to the meeting but saw you through the window and decided it was probably better to let you catch some rest. These boys will talk about what happened and plan for what comes next a few more times before you leave, I'm certain. They live for after-action reports and strategy sessions." She rolled her eyes, smiling, even as the man next to her covered her hand with his.

"All the better to keep you safe, my dear," he added, sending a grin toward Maria that was more than intimate.

Maria swatted at his hand playfully and turned back to Mandy. "Don't mind my husband. Jesse has a Big Bad Wolf complex."

Husband. That answered a question Mandy hadn't even realized she'd had. Moore had called Maria his *mate*. So, *mates* were spouses in the shifter world. Interesting. And his first name, apparently, was Jesse.

"Sorry you missed out on the debrief,

Ranger Clarke," Jesse spoke in a more serious tone. "But I bowed to my wife's wisdom when she suggested you needed a bit of recovery time. She knows humans better than I ever will. Especially of the female variety."

Mandy wasn't sure how to take that but decided not to be offended. "I'm sorry to have missed it, as well. I haven't been sleeping well, and it's been a while since I was in a shoot-out. It all sort of took me by surprise," she admitted. "And, please, call me Mandy."

Jesse nodded respectfully. "Call me Jesse," he invited. "By all accounts, you handled yourself very well, indeed. I suspect the old instincts never really go away, even when you choose not to use them for a while. William mentioned you were a police officer?"

Mandy nodded. She wondered how to change the subject but couldn't figure a way without insulting these people who had already done so much for her, and Wil, and the others.

"In Seattle," she confirmed, nodding as if it was no big deal. "I was shot in pursuit of a man that had killed twice already, I'm sorry to say. He cornered me, and well, after that, I decided to turn in my badge and seek the peace of the mountains." She tried to make light of the ordeal that had changed her forever. "I knew things were different up there, but I didn't realize just how different. I guess I should've figured out something was up when that giant wolf would hang out with William at night. That was no ordinary wolf." She smiled and shook her head at her own self-delusion.

Jesse grinned. "You've got that right. The Alpha was watching over William. I had a phone conversation with him a few hours ago and made him aware of William's past and how much we, in the Special Forces community, look up to him. I told that Alpha that I owe him one."

Mandy suspected, from the tone, that this man didn't hand out favors easily. She also realized that, if he was the Alpha, as they called it, of this group, he was a very powerful man, indeed. Every man in the room—and it was a big room, filled with people—looked like some sort of super-soldier. If not for Maria's presence, along with a few other women, here and there, she would have thought she was on a military base. Some of the other women were wearing bright colors and civilian dress. They were bright spots amongst all the dark fatigues and worn-in uniform pieces with no insignia.

There were quite a few women dressed like soldiers, as well, she noticed. In among the men, there were tall, svelte women wearing cargo pants and T-shirts, just like their male counterparts. But there were definitely other women who weren't part of the military group, who seemed to be girlfriends or wives. Even some mothers with children, who sat among the larger group. They were clearly part of the bigger group, though fulfilling a slightly different role. It was fascinating to Mandy. They all seemed to function as one big happy family regardless of the role they played in the basic structure of the group. It was surprisingly egalitarian for a military setting.

"It's me that owes him," William put in from Jesse's other side. "And I have some ideas of how to thank him and his Pack for looking after me for the past few months, that I will implement as soon as I get where I'm going."

"They'll appreciate whatever you have in mind, I'm sure," Jesse said gently. "Nevertheless, his Pack has a favor from the Wraiths, and me, personally, in reserve."

"That's good of you, Major," William said solemnly. "They're good people on that mountain. I'm going to miss them."

Jesse nodded. "I'm certain they'll miss you, as well. I thought you might be interested to know that I arranged with Norman to install one of my guys up on that mountain, in your old job, for now. We've cleared it with the Park Service and set up a false paper trail that will stand up to just about any scrutiny. I wanted eyes up there in case the people who are after your son and his comrades come sniffing around again. Though, after their losses today, I suspect they won't try that route again." Jesse had a grim smile of satisfaction on his face. "Losing five mages all at once. That had to hurt their brotherhood. Even if these were lower-level magic users who had to work as a group to do what they did."

Mandy realized he spoke as if he knew the group to which the attackers had belonged. That was an interesting idea. She hadn't thought they were part of an organized group, but it made sense. That much coordination took money and power, which often came with organized crime. Not the mafia, of course, but some kind of magical version. The thought gave her pause. She'd have to learn more about this hidden world and its people and organizations.

"Does this group have a name?" she asked cautiously. She still wasn't sure what was allowable and what wasn't in shifter culture.

"We'll await confirmation from the Lords, but this has all the earmarks of a *Venifucus* strike," Jesse told her. The name was unfamiliar but sounded sort of Latin to her.

"Is it all right if I ask who or what the *Venifucus* are?" Mandy ventured further. "I like to know my enemy."

Jesse eyed her and nodded. "The *Venifucus* are an ancient order dedicated to evil. In particular, they are working toward the return of their leader, what they call their *Mater Priori*. She's an ancient fey sorceress named Elspeth. Many on our side call her the Destroyer. The Dark Ages? That was the last time she was in this realm, trying to take over and destroy everything we hold dear. The forces of Light fought her off and banished her to the farthest realms. Everybody thought that her minions in the *Venifucus* had disbanded and that the order was no more, but we've learned differently in recent years. They're back, if they ever left, and they're as vicious as ever."

"There are those who say Elspeth has already returned," Seth put in from across the table. His voice was like velvet, his tone mysterious and his words tinged with just the tiniest bit of an exotic accent.

Jesse nodded gravely. "I've heard the rumors, and more than that, I'm aware of several attempts by several different groups of her followers to usurp sources of power in order to generate the amount of magic needed to pull her back into this realm. The attempts I know about were stopped, but that doesn't mean our side caught them all. They might have been successful somewhere else, in some other part of the world."

"Too true, my friend," Seth said, agreeing with Jesse's dire words. "It is all too possible that the rumors are true, and we will see increase in activity from her followers once again."

Mandy'd had no idea there was an ancient battle between good and evil going on without most of the world's population being aware of it. Somehow, only the magical races knew what was really going on, and they were fighting on behalf of everyone. It didn't seem right to her, but then again, what could normal people do against magic? She'd been as useless as everyone else when that magical whammy had landed her on her butt earlier today. If not for Wil's incredible ability with that lightning, they all probably would have died right then and there.

There was a pause before Jesse turned back to Mandy. His tone was somber when he spoke. "I'm sorry to have to be the one to tell you about all this. I wish the news was better and that we weren't in the middle of an epic struggle, but those are the cards we've been dealt, and that's what we'll all have to deal with in the coming days, months and maybe even years. The armies are gathering, and skirmishes are already happening. Whether or not the final battle is near or not, I just can't say, but you better believe we're all getting ready. Now that you know about all this, you should probably do the same."

"To whatever extent I can," she replied, "I will. Thanks for the information."

Jesse nodded respectfully. "That's what we do, first and foremost," he said. "We're an intel gathering operation at our heart, though we do get into the action from time to time, when necessary." Jesse sat back in his chair and looked around the table at Liam, Rick, William and then back to her and Wil. "I heard back from your father, Liam, before coming down to dinner. He's arranged transport for you all tomorrow afternoon. Our helo will take you to an airstrip in Nebraska. A jet will pick you up there and take you the rest of the way."

The men had a few logistical questions for Jesse and the discussion of the following day's arrangements got a bit more detailed. Mandy tuned them out a bit as she mulled over what Jesse had told her. She ate her dinner, enjoying the tender steak and mashed potatoes as she let the conversation go on around her.

When dinner was over, Wil walked her back to her cabin. The winding pathway was dark under the trees, but Wil had a small light with which he kept them on the right path. She was glad of the escort, because, despite her months spent on the mountain in Montana, she was still really a city girl at heart. Navigating in the woods at night wasn't her forte.

The darkness around them reminded her a little of the dark night she'd been shot in the line of duty. For the first time, the idea of talking about it didn't fill her with dread. In fact, she wanted Wil to know her deep dark secret. Maybe because she had learned some highly classified things about him today. Or, maybe, it was just Wil. Something about him inspired confidences. She knew he would never betray her trust, though how she was so certain, she didn't know. Whatever provoked the impulse, she followed her instincts and broached a subject she'd thought she would never willingly bring up with anyone.

"You know I was a cop," she said quietly as they made their way down the forest path in the darkness, "and that I was shot in the line of duty by a man who had already killed two other people."

"Yeah, that had to be rough," Wil replied.

"What I haven't said is that while I was down, he...uh...assaulted me," she admitted, looking down, unable to meet Wil's gaze.

"He beat you up?"

"The intent was sexual," she clarified, finding her backbone, "but he didn't get too far before my backup arrived. Still, the whole incident really shook me. I spent a lot of time in the hospital, and then a lot at home, recuperating. When it was time to go back to work, I…"

"I think I understand," Wil said in a comforting, low tone.

"I feel like such a coward for running away, but at the time, it's what I needed to do," she told him, hearing the truth in her words, even as she spoke them. Something inside her had changed in the time she'd been on the mountain. Some spark of gumption had returned, and she hadn't even realized it until the crisis today.

"We all need to regroup sometimes," Wil replied after a moment. "The important thing is that you keep fighting your way back."

She looked at him, seeing the earnest expression on his face. He really did seem to understand. Of course, he'd probably seen and done things as a soldier that were comparable— and, perhaps, even more violent—than what she'd been through. Maybe he really did understand in a way her non-cop friends just hadn't been able to comprehend.

Wil was so easy to talk to. It hadn't been as difficult as she'd expected to tell him what had happened to her. He'd made it easy, somehow. Of course, she was in a much better place mentally, now, than she had been even just a few weeks ago.

Her reaction to the firefight had surprised her in a good way. She'd been all business. The old Mandy, from before the attack. She'd responded well, and she was proud of herself for keeping cool under fire and everything that had come after. Even the revelations of magic and that Wil had superpowers hadn't thrown her too far off her stride. Maybe she really was coming back from the trauma. Maybe there was hope she would be the woman she had once been. Scratch that. Maybe she would be even better.

A new creation, risen from the ashes of the old. A phoenix who was stronger and better able to deal with life's dramas.

Yeah. That's what she wanted. She wouldn't be happy with just being as good as she was. She wanted to be even better. More daring. More adventurous. More courageous.

She looked speculatively at Wil. If she was going to become that woman, she might as well start now. They were almost to her cabin. She decided, then and there, she was going to invite Wil inside, and damn the torpedoes, she was going full steam ahead!

CHAPTER FIFTEEN

She stepped closer to him in the darkness, going toe to toe, invading his personal space. She met his gaze. She was just able to make out his strong features and the gleam of his eyes. He looked a bit surprised, at first, but his expression soon turned to something more receptive…and sexy.

"Would you like to come inside with me?" she asked in a near-breathless voice. She hadn't been this bold in too long a time. She liked the empowering feeling of being her own woman once again.

"If I go into that guest cabin with you, Mandy, I'll warn you now… I won't want to leave until morning." His low voice rumbled through her, setting her nerve endings alight with desire.

She smiled up at him. "Good," she told him, enjoying the flare of awareness in his eyes. "I really don't want you to leave too soon."

He raised his hand to stroke her hair then cupped her cheek tenderly. "Are you sure?"

She nodded slowly. "I want this," she replied simply. "I want you. Tonight. For as long as we have. I don't want to let this chance slip away. We have this night out of time. I think we should enjoy it to the fullest."

"A night out of time," he mused. "I like that. It really does feel that way, doesn't it?" He moved his hand away from her face and slid it around to her waist, drawing her against his hard body. "Just so long as we both understand, I'm not sure what the future holds, right now. A lot is up in the air, and it's not just up to me to decide what happens next."

"I know that," she reassured him. "I know you're committed to the Army and that my own future is uncertain, now that I've learned what I've learned and saw what I saw. I get it. But, you know, I have to believe that the future is always uncertain. Ours is just a bit more uncertain than most, right now." She gave him a rueful smile. "Still, we have tonight. That's a fact. I don't want to waste it being alone."

"Then, what are we waiting for?" He let her go, but only to turn around so she could walk beside him as they crossed the final steps to the guest cabin and went inside.

She had left a single dim light on inside the cabin, and that was enough. Anything brighter would kill the mood that was building between them. She led him to the bed, which wasn't far, considering how small the cabin actually was, and reached up to place one hand at the nape of his neck, encouraging him to lean down so they could kiss.

She was nervous, but in a good way, as their lips met, and time seemed to stand still. His lips caressed hers in an unhurried exploration of desire.

She pushed at his shirt, wanting the fabric between them gone. He seemed to get the message, taking a moment to strip off the olive T-shirt that had been making her think naughty thoughts since the moment she'd seen him. It fit just a bit snugly, outlining Wil's amazing musculature in a way that made her mouth water.

He was more than handsome. He was physically devastating, but the kind heart and courageous actions were what had completely won her over. He was the total package. A man who respected her and whom she could respect...and love?

If she was being honest with herself, she was sliding quickly down that slope, falling head over heels in love with a man whose life was so complicated that she had serious doubt there could be room in it for her. She was kidding herself if she thought there would definitely be something lasting out of this brief encounter. He had obligations and all sorts of changes going on in his life. She understood. She'd been down a similar road and knew that sometimes, no matter how much you might wish things were different, you just had to play the cards you were dealt and hope for the best.

In Wil's case, the hand he was playing was a doozy. New amazing superpowers and the discovery of magic in the world had to make him wonder where he fit in to all of it. She knew his superiors were scrambling to figure out the same thing. He was a soldier, and with the new abilities he had gained, he had a duty to figure out how best to use them in service of his country, and the forces of good.

It was a hell of a lot of responsibility, but she had confidence in him. He would find a path forward for himself and his unit. He'd be part of the fight. It was just who he was. Whether or not there'd be room for an ongoing relationship with her in his life... Well, that was another matter altogether. She refused to think about it anymore. Not when she could run her hands over his skin and feel the muscle that had tantalized her for the past hours.

Not when she could lean forward and lick his neck, learning the taste and texture of him, the scent and feel of his body against hers. Putting her thoughts into action, she began a tantalizing exploration, allowing her desire free reign. He seemed to like it if his shivers and groans were anything to go by.

She sank down onto her knees, unbuttoning and unzipping his pants in a daring move she felt compelled to try. Pushing at the fabric of his waistband, she took down his trousers and undies in one smooth pull, freeing him to her gaze...and her touch.

Mandy wrapped one hand around him, learning the feel and heat of him. Gazing upward to meet his eyes, she saw he was watching her intently. She imagined—or, maybe, it wasn't entirely her imagination—that she saw little sparks of lightning in his gaze. The power of him enticed her. Touching him so intimately made her feel almost invincible as he let her do as she wished.

Encouraged by the desire in his eyes, she lowered her head and licked the tip of him, satisfied when he groaned. She amused herself, teasing him and learning what he liked. He allowed it, though she could feel the slight tremble in his muscled thighs as she sucked him deep into her mouth.

He bent over, and she realized her time for play was at an end. He put his hands under her arms and lifted her up and away from him, turning in one swift move and placing her on the bed. He came down beside her and began undressing her with fingers that weren't entirely steady. She'd brought him to an edge, and he was holding back, turning the tables, waiting on his own pleasure so as to bring her along with him.

She learned quickly that Wil was a considerate lover, as well as an expert at making her body sing with excitement. He undressed her with care, his big hands gentle on her body. He kissed each bit of skin he exposed, pausing for a long time as he uncovered her breasts, licking and sucking on her body in ways that made her writhe in ecstasy.

159

When she was bare, he got rid of the rest of his clothing, which wasn't much, thanks to her earlier work, and came down over her on the thankfully large bed. The shifters had equipped this small cabin with a nice wide bed that was big enough for a man of Wil's stature with plenty of room to spare. It made for a nice romping ground as Wil set off on an expedition of discovery and enticement, coaxing her responses with well-placed caresses.

She lost track of time, and when he finally joined his body to hers, she was more than ready to find the ultimate pleasure. It took only a few thrusts from his powerful body to send her into orbit. She came with a sobbing cry of relief. Wil kept going, pushing her through her first orgasm into a new round of suspense. He played her body with his like a master plays a violin—all smooth glides of bow on string, of his body on hers, their passions united in straining towards a new crescendo.

He built her passion to such a height that she almost touched the stars when she came a second time, some moments later. This time, he was with her, his groans of completion complementing her cries of passion strained to new limits. She'd never climbed so high. She'd never known lovemaking could be this catastrophic. This incredible. This life-altering.

If she'd thought she was halfway in love with Wil before now, this experience let her know, in no uncertain terms, that her body, at least, was all the way in his thrall. Wil, alone, of the men she'd known intimately, could take her places she hadn't known existed. He could easily make her his love slave, she thought with a wry grin at her own expense.

For an independent woman like Mandy, it was a scandalous thought. As she came down off the greatest climax she'd ever known, she let her mind drift. There would be time later—much later—to think about the future. For now, she just wanted to bask.

Wil pulled the blanket over them both a few minutes later, settling them both in the big bed. He kept her next to him, his arm around her waist, spooning her as if he didn't want to let her go. She liked that and fell into a doze with what had to be a sappy smile on her face.

He woke her twice more in the night to make love. Each time was an education. She'd thought he couldn't do any better than that first amazing experience, but she'd been wrong. Oh, so wrong.

Her pleasure just got better and better, each time they were together. Finally, just before dawn, he snuggled her back into his arms, and they slept for another couple of hours before they had to be up and ready for action.

The next day, they boarded the same helicopter they'd arrived in, and Jesse Moore accompanied them again. The flight was a bit longer than their previous journey, but not by much. They landed in Nebraska, in the middle of what looked like somebody's cornfield, though there was a hangar and a few small planes on the ground near a paved and marked runway. They landed in an open area next to the hangar, and to Mandy's surprise, the pilots shut the chopper down. It seemed the mercenaries were going to stay for a while.

Jesse accompanied their group down the ramp while the pilots busied themselves refueling the chopper and dealing with a few folks in overalls who had come out of the hangar to meet them. They looked friendly enough as Mandy watched them exchange greetings from a distance, which she thought boded well. She followed the group into the hangar, blinking as her eyes adjusted from the bright sunshine of outside to the shaded interior of the large building.

She noted a few planes parked inside the hangar, among them a jet that gleamed shiny white with a blue stripe running down the side. This was no commercial jet, but a civilian one. A *luxury* civilian jet, at that. Mandy had been expecting some sort of military transport, but she didn't see anything like that in the area. Maybe they'd have to wait for their plane to arrive.

A blond man came down the stairs of the luxury jet and smiled at Jesse Moore, moving to intercept. It looked to Mandy like the man from the fancy jet knew Jesse and was pleased to see him. They shook hands as the rest of the group stopped walking and waited to see what was going on. After a moment, Jesse turned to William and introduced his friend.

"Lieutenant Colonel Owens, this is Hank Schleichender. We served together for a bit, but now, he works exclusively for Pepard Industries. He'll be flying you to your destination from here," Jesse informed William, though he spoke loud enough for the rest of them to hear.

"Colonel Owens, it's an honor, sir," Hank said, stretching out his hand to shake William's.

"Call me William, son. I'm retired," Senior replied. "So, just why is a reclusive billionaire doing favors for Uncle Sam?" William asked quietly. "Or should I just not mention it?"

Hank smiled. "You can ask, but all I'm prepared to say is that the Alpha here," he nodded toward Jesse, "called in a favor. As did a certain admiral we all know." Hank shook his head. "Seems my employer is ready, willing, and able to lend all available assistance to the groups currently stationed on Plum Island," Hank replied quietly, revealing in a few words the full extent of his—and his employer's—knowledge.

That the reclusive billionaire, Mark Pepard, not only knew about shifters but was willing to help in the battle they were currently fighting against evil was eye-opening. What was more, the implications of Hank's words meant Pepard also knew that Wil and Rick's unit was on Plum Island and that they were slightly different than the shifters who were already stationed there.

Jesse lightened the mood by introducing everyone, one by one. Mandy stuck by Wil's side and heard what he said to Hank as the others gathered around Jesse for a moment.

"I recognize you. You flew my unit out of

the Middle East more than a few years back. You were in the Air Force back then, though. Spec Ops. Am I right?" Wil and Hank shook hands as Mandy looked on.

"That was me," Hank agreed. "Like your father, I retired some time ago. I've been flying for Pepard ever since." Hank turned to acknowledge Mandy. "You're the park ranger?"

"Amanda Clarke." She offered her hand to the pilot.

"Pleasure to meet you, Officer Clarke." Hank turned, and Mandy saw the woman coming down the stairs of the jet. "Ah. And this is my mate, Tracy, and our daughter, Emma." Mandy noted how Hank's entire face lit up when he saw his family.

Tracy was carrying a sleepy little girl in her arms but was wearing the neat uniform of a pilot, same as her husband. Or mate. That's what he'd called her. Realization dawned. Hank was a shifter. Maybe Tracy and little Emma, too. Mandy tried to hide her reaction but knew she was probably staring, so she smiled and offered her greetings to the woman and child.

"Hi, I'm Mandy," she said, waving to the little girl who was watching them out of sleepy eyes. Mandy stepped closer to the two females and let the men stand a little apart so they could continue sizing each other up and comparing military histories. "You're a pilot, too?" Mandy asked of the woman.

"Absolutely. My dad owns an airport, so I figured I'd learn to fly," Tracy said. "Just about everybody in my family flies, and little Em will probably learn when she's old enough. She's fascinated by airplanes, aren't you, sweetie?" Tracy bent down to kiss her daughter's forehead, and the little girl nodded then tucked her head into her mother's shoulder. "Sorry. She's had a long day. She'll probably sleep through the hop to New York."

"I think it's awesome that you can travel as a family even while you work," Mandy said, thinking that Pepard must not be the usual sort of employer.

"You can say that again," Tracy replied, then took a step away. "You're welcome to board whenever you like. We're just going to take a short walk while we're on the ground, then Em and I will be back aboard. Sissy is working with us today as steward, so if you need anything in the cabin, she can get it for you."

"Thanks," Mandy said as Tracy and her daughter moved away. Wil seemed to notice and moved back to Mandy's side.

"You about ready to go aboard?" he asked in a quiet voice.

Mandy took a last look around the hangar. There wasn't much else to see, and she was more than ready to check out the inside of the jet. She nodded and headed up the stairs. Wil was right behind her.

The interior of the jet was sumptuous. In leather-upholstered seating that was large enough for the biggest men in their group to be comfortable, Mandy felt as if she was sitting on a cloud. She and Wil were sitting next to each other, with his dad and Rick facing them in a conversational grouping with a removable table in the center of their group of seats. Liam sat to one side, chatting with Tracy and playing with little Emma until she fell asleep about twenty minutes after they'd reached cruising altitude.

Tracy had come out of the cockpit once they'd levelled out and surprised Mandy by staying for a while. Once Emma had fallen asleep, she carried her sleeping daughter back to the cockpit. Sissy must have seen Mandy's bemused gaze because she paused at Mandy's side while delivering a round of drinks to the group.

"When Hank brought Tracy and Emma in, they expanded the cockpit area of this jet. There's room up there for Emma's cot and a little jump seat where she can strap in for take offs and landings. When Hank is flying a job where he can bring the family along, this is the jet they use," Sissy told Mandy.

"That's pretty amazing," Mandy commented. "I never knew Pepard was so caring of his employees."

Sissy tilted her head in a sort of feline way. "Mark's the best Alpha there is," she answered simply. "He cares for us because we're all family."

CHAPTER SIXTEEN

Mandy realized that Sissy must also be a shifter, and her eyes widened as she smiled. "I'm still very new to all this."

Sissy smiled back. "It's okay. You'll learn. You're going to have to if you keep hanging around with this bunch." She picked up the empties and raised her voice a little to be heard by the entire group. "Just let me know if you need anything else."

The rest of the flight passed in a blur. The men chatted most of the way while Mandy's head spun. She had really fallen down the rabbit hole and was just starting to get the lay of the land in this new reality. It would take time, as Sissy had suggested, to learn all she needed to know. The question was, would she have the time? Would she be allowed to stick with Wil and his unit? Or would she be summarily dismissed once the danger was past?

Not by Wil. Mandy knew Wil wasn't that kind of guy.

When they landed in New York, they used an airport specifically for smaller planes out on the East End of Long Island. Theirs was one of the larger craft on the ground, but by no means the most luxurious. This part of the island sported enormous mansions where lots of the rich and famous spent their weekends away from the hustle and bustle of Manhattan, which was only a few hours away by ground transport. Less, if you had your own helicopter, of course.

As they descended from the jet, a stretched-out Hummer pulled up, and four people got out. Mandy recognized the movie star Sullivan Lane first. She was even more gorgeous in person than she was on the screen. Then, she realized one of the men was Mark Pepard, himself. He was clearly with the other woman in the small group, and the other man was helping Sullivan Lane with her luggage and seemed to be with her.

Two couples, she realized belatedly. Two very powerful, very rich couples.

Mandy wasn't used to rubbing elbows with such high society. She hung back, even as Liam stepped forward to greet them. Mandy was surprised when the four newcomers stopped to chat, seeming at ease being introduced to the others in her group. When it was her turn, she stuttered a little but managed to not make a complete fool of herself meeting such important people.

"Thanks very much for the use of your jet," William said to Mark Pepard. Unlike Mandy, William seemed at ease. He even had a twinkle in his eye as he smiled at Sullivan Lane. The old coot.

"Happy to help, Colonel Owens. Good to see you looking so well. Of course, I've been hearing some interesting things about the new unit on Kinkaid's island." Those shrewd eyes turned to Rick and Wil, a sly smile on the eccentric billionaire's face. "I hope you'll bring my best regards to your unit commander. I'd like to consider us allies, of a sort."

"We'll be sure to tell him," Wil replied. "As my father said, thank you very much for the use of your airplane, and for sending Hank and his family."

Pepard grinned. "That Hank certainly gets around. He's been a very good ambassador from our Clan to the Special Forces community. He is living proof that you can have your feet in both worlds and still lead a great life full of adventure and now, family."

Pepard's attention was drawn to the woman and child now coming down the steps of the plane. The little girl was jumping down each step and didn't stop jumping once she reached the ground. She looked around, saw Mark and let go of her mother's hand to run to him. When she was still five feet from the man, she took a running leap that would have been impossible for a normal human child, but her trust and daring was rewarded when Mark bent down to catch her mid-air and lift her high in his arms as he laughed at her antics.

"Little Miss Emma loves her Alpha," Mark's wife, Shelly, put in. She smiled at the girl then turned to address Mandy. "All the children do, actually. It's like they sense he's protecting them all, all the time."

Mandy knew her eyes were widening, but the revelations just kept coming. The reclusive billionaire businessman was an *Alpha*? Were there shifters everywhere, living in secret among ordinary people? Mandy shook her head.

"Sorry, ma'am. My mind continues to struggle with the idea that you all have been living in secret, all this time, and I never even guessed," Mandy said, probably being a bit too blunt, but it was her nature to be plain-spoken.

"Oh, not me. Not really. I'm not a shifter. Neither is Sully, actually. But our husbands are, and yeah, I understand that it's a lot to take in," Shelly replied not unkindly. "Of course, your friends can do some pretty amazing stuff, too, if rumors are to be believed." Shelly looked at Rick and Wil, then back to Mandy. "There are all kinds of magic all around us. You just have to see it once to realize it's been there, hiding in plain sight, all along."

Mandy realized the truth of Shelly's words. After the recent revelations, she would never look at the world the same way again.

After a bit more small talk, the two groups exchanged places. The two couples went into the jet while Mandy's group got into the very large vehicle. The custom behemoth had been stretched by a body shop and refitted with a luxurious interior. There was sumptuous leather upholstery and all sorts of conveniences, including a small refrigerator stocked with cold drinks. The driver lowered the privacy window between the driver and passenger compartment, and Wil and Rick both started grinning.

"Jeeves," Rick said in a loud voice. "Nice to see you behind the wheel."

"What do you think of the wheels? This baby is armored. And the drinks and snacks are for you guys, if you want them. I'll have us to the boat ramp in two shakes." The man started the vehicle moving and had them off the tarmac quickly.

"A British chauffeur?" William asked, his eyebrow rising, even as humor sparked in his eyes.

"Only half-British, sir, though I grew up mostly across the pond and haven't been able to shake the accent completely," Jeeves clarified as he expertly steered the long vehicle through a series of turns ending at an on-ramp.

"Dad, Jeeves is a member of our unit. Don't let the accent fool you," Wil said as they rolled along, picking up speed as Jeeves steered them onto a highway. "Dad, Mandy, our driver today is Lieutenant Jeff Penworthy."

"At your service," Jeeves said, looking briefly into the rearview mirror then back to the road.

"Nice to meet you, Jeff," Mandy said. "Thanks for coming to pick us up."

"You're very welcome, though to be honest,

when I saw this Hummer, I couldn't resist. Getting to chat with Sullivan Lane was pretty darn cool, too," Jeeves admitted.

"How did that happen?" Rick asked.

"This is one of Pepard's vehicles. He drove it to the boat ramp. Though, I guess his bodyguard, Nick Balam, did the driving. They came across on the boat to have a powwow with Commander Kinkaid and our captain. I volunteered to go back with them and get you. Pepard said they were leaving the Hummer in the secure lot at the boat dock so it would be available for us or Kinkaid's people to use. Cool, huh?" Jeeves enthused. "It'll come in handy when... Oh." Jeeves stopped talking suddenly and frowned a bit.

"Still not telling us what's going to happen next?" Wil asked, rolling his eyes at his teammate.

"Rosie thinks it's for the best," Jeeves defended himself. "And I agree. It's not good to know too much about the future. Some things need to unfold naturally. However, I will say that it's very nice to have both Colonel Owens and Officer Clarke joining the team. You both have important functions to perform within our unit and for the good of all who serve."

Wil must have seen the confusion on Mandy's face. He sighed and explained, "Jeeves here can see the future. So can his wife, Rosie. The two of them like to pick and choose what they reveal to the rest of us," Wil said.

"Unless you really need to know, of course.

We've managed to avoid a lot of problems by warning you all beforehand when something bad is going to happen, haven't we?" Jeeves asked.

"Okay, you've got a point," Wil conceded. "It just feels like you hold out more than you explain lately, but I won't quibble. You've got to figure out how to deal with that freaky new ability of yours, just like the rest of us."

They bantered a bit more, but Mandy was taken aback by the idea that the man who could see the future saw a role for her in Wil's unit. In Wil's life? Was he not saying that Wil and she would be working—and maybe a whole lot more—together? A glimmer of hope took hold in her heart at the thought that would not be denied.

The boat, when Mandy saw it, turned out to be a military vessel with armament, painted in Coast Guard regalia, though it was pretty clear the crew manning it were Navy, not Coast Guard, based on their uniforms and insignia. They greeted Liam as an old friend and were less enthusiastic, yet still friendly, towards Rick and Wil. Their attitude toward Wil's dad was almost reverent, which was how most Special Forces folks acted around him, Mandy had some to realize.

She'd known William was something special, but she hadn't realized just how much of a reputation he'd had among his peers. He was, apparently, something of a legend among the military folks in the know, which impressed her all over again. She already loved the old man for the stoic courage he'd displayed in facing his own imminent death. He was the kind of man a person could look up to in so many ways, and since meeting his son, she realized Wil was a real chip off the old block. He might not be a Special Forces legend, but he was dealing with some amazing things and still keeping it all together and doing his best to protect and serve.

That was something she, as a former police officer, really admired. She'd had that same drive to serve others and would still be in the job she'd loved today if not for her bad experience.

The boat ride across to the small island was pleasant enough. It was a beautiful day to be on the water. She just wished she felt more certain about her destiny and had less questions about her immediate future. Would she be able to be with Wil? She very much doubted it. They were going, after all, to a military base. She didn't think fraternization—if that's what they called it—would be allowed.

Much to her surprise, a mixed group of civilians and uniformed people waited for them on the dock. Liam, Rick and Wil saluted the two older men who were clearly officers. Once they were told to be *at ease*, introductions were made. The man in the naval uniform turned out to be Commander Kinkaid, Liam's father, and the Green Beret Captain was Rick and Wil's commanding officer, Captain Haliwell.

She'd sort of expected someone from the command structure to want to meet the new arrivals, but the fact that they'd come out to the boat dock was significant. Both men treated William with the utmost respect, which warmed Mandy's heart. It was good to see the old man doing so well and rejoining the human race among people who valued him.

They were both polite to her, as well. Captain Haliwell was a big man with a strong handshake, but he didn't overwhelm her with his iron grip the way some men sometimes did. He was polite and considerate, and much to her surprise, he'd brought his wife, Casey, with him. That wasn't standard military procedure, she was sure, but the clearly civilian woman in the pretty dress made from yellow daisy fabric was kindness itself. She greeted Mandy like an old friend and promised to show her the *girlie* amenities she'd insisted they put in the barracks building later.

While Mandy wasn't sure what to make of that, Casey's description of a spa area for the ladies made Mandy very curious, indeed. It had been a long time since she'd treated herself to a spa.

After the introductions were made, Commander Kinkaid took charge of William, inviting the old man to his office for a discussion. Liam was ordered to report in two hours for a mission debrief, and he took off with a casual goodbye to the group.

Rick and Wil received the same order for the debrief, and to Mandy's surprise, she was invited to join them, as well. She saw a hint of respect in Captain Haliwell's eyes as he made the request that she really liked. He was a strong man, but he clearly commanded the respect of his men. Mandy suspected that was not just because of his position as an officer, but rather, because of his leadership. She liked that.

They began walking toward a building in the distance that Casey called the barracks. She walked next to Mandy with Captain Haliwell on her other side and Rick and Wil following along behind. They were going to have a few minutes to clean up and compose themselves before the debrief, during which, Casey would show Mandy her quarters and give her the basic tour of the available amenities before leaving her to settle in and freshen up.

When they reached the building, the group split up. Rick and Wil peeled off to go to their quarters while Casey took charge of Mandy. Captain Haliwell left them with a reminder of the meeting time and a brief kiss for his wife.

"So, are you and Wil an item?" Casey wasted no time in asking. Mandy could feel her cheeks heat with a flush.

"Uh…" She was surprisingly tongue-tied.

Casey smiled. "It's just that, if you're going to bunk with him, I'll put you in the room at the end of the corridor nearest his quarters. If not, I can put you in a room with a better view. It's your call."

"Um…" Mandy rolled the dice. If this was a way to gather intel and get Wil in trouble, they'd just have to deal with the fallout. "The end of the corridor sounds good," she said, mentally crossing her fingers and hoping for the best.

"That's great!" Casey squealed a bit, surprising Mandy, then led the way up the stairs, talking as she went. "I was hoping both of them would find someone. At least one of them has. Thank goodness. Two lonelier men I've never met. They all try to be so stoic, but this change has really hit them all pretty hard. A few have found someone to share the burden, but not enough, in my opinion. I have a goal to get them all happily married off. Like they were my kids or something," she snorted, laughing as she mounted the last step. "Do you like children?" Casey asked, turning suddenly to Mandy.

When she nodded, Casey went right on talking as she led the way to the left side of the stairs, which were centrally located in the building.

"Hal and I have a little girl. So far, none of the others have had kids. I'm hoping she'll have some playmates before too much longer." Casey looked over her shoulder and giggled. "Any chance you're pregnant?"

Mandy was shocked by the question and unable to answer before Casey started laughing.

"If you could see the look on your face," she said between gales of laughter. "It's okay. I didn't mean to shock you. I'm just on a bit of a mission to make this place less of a military installation and more of a home. More kids will help with that."

"But it is a military installation," Mandy

couldn't help but point out.

Casey's steps slowed. "Yeah, I know." She turned to face Mandy fully. "But this isn't a normal situation. We can't leave. The unit's being targeted. The unit's family is being targeted. Until that ends, we're stuck here, and I, for one, didn't sign up for the Army or even the Navy. I'm making the best of this and reminding everybody that they're people first, super-soldiers second."

Mandy thought about that for a second. "People first," she repeated. "I like that. I can see how, with their new abilities, they might lose sight of that."

"There's a lot that makes them different from regular folks. There always was, even before they were changed. The superhero powers only made that gulf wider, and it's my mission to bridge the chasm. They need us as much as we need them. Their emotional needs didn't change, only their abilities to do things that the rest of us can't. If that makes sense."

Mandy nodded as they started walking again. "It makes a lot of sense, actually. I'm glad Wil's got someone like you looking out for him and his unit."

Casey stopped in front of the first door near the end of the corridor they had just entered and smiled at Mandy. "Thanks," she said. "This is your room. Even if you don't sleep here, it's a place to put your stuff." She opened the door and ushered Mandy inside. "As you can see, there's a desk and a little home office area. Some of us use it for arts and crafts. I've taken up sewing, for example." She gestured toward the pretty dress she was wearing.

"You made that?" Mandy was impressed.

Casey beamed. "I did. It's not a super complicated pattern, but I'm starting to make my own designs, and some of them actually are pretty comfortable."

"That's amazing," Mandy enthused. "It's a lovely dress. Very flattering, and the colors complement your hair and eyes."

"Thank you," Casey said, smiling once more. Mandy could tell already that Casey was a very positive person who smiled more often than she frowned. If this was the surrogate mother the unit had looking after it, they were in good hands.

CHAPTER SEVENTEEN

Casey left after pointing out where the facilities were located and giving Mandy directions on how to get to the meeting room where the debriefing would be held. Mandy took a few minutes to just sit down and relax, looking out the room's single window. The view wasn't bad. She could see the water and some trees leading up to it. The shoreline here looked like hard-packed sand and rocks, and even as she watched, a late-afternoon jogger in sweats with Navy emblems on them ran past and farther down the beach, out of sight.

Mandy got up and checked out the closets, finding that some basic amenities had been stocked for the occupant of the room. This included a set of light gray sweats with no logos that would fit reasonably well, and a little bag of toiletries that had Casey's feminine touch written all over them. There was even an artificial daisy attached to the handle with a hand-written welcome tag.

Casey took a few of the items with her down the hall to the promised bathroom and opened the door to find what looked like an indoor oasis of calm. She could feel the stress of the day melting away as she contemplated whether or not she had enough time for a quick shower before the meeting. Deciding to take advantage of the hour and change she had left, she located towels and a robe on the shelves that were clearly there for anybody who needed them, and locked herself into one of the spacious shower stalls.

It was refreshing to wash away the miles they had flown that day and let the hot water soothe her spirit. The moister air at this altitude was something she'd missed living in the mountains. The adjustment to the thinner, drier air up there had taken a while, but she found she was enjoying herself back at sea level and took to it like the proverbial duck—or seagull, since they seemed to be plentiful on this island—to water.

The debrief was straightforward for the most part. The men led the way, describing the series of events in cold detail. It only started to get surreal when they got to the part where the animals joined in on their side, and then, it got downright freaky when they described how the five *mages* had entered the fray. Of course, Liam seemed most comfortable discussing such things, though Rick and Wil were clearly starting to be more at ease about magical stuff. For Mandy, it was still quite shocking, even though she'd lived to tell the tale.

She went over events from her point of view, when asked. Captain Haliwell casually mentioned that he'd be talking to Wil's father separately, just to get his version of events for the official Top-Secret record.

"Personally, and for your sake, Wil, I'm hoping your dad will accept the offer Commander Kinkaid is making him, probably as we speak," Captain Haliwell said casually as they ended their meeting.

"They're going to offer him a training position?" Wil asked, hope clear in his tone.

Captain Haliwell nodded. "We could all use instruction from someone like him," he replied. "I know you've taught us what he taught you, but I'm sure there are things still hidden up his sleeve that we could benefit from. And, even if our unit already knows all his tricks, the shifters don't, and they tend to rely, in my opinion, a little too much on their animal gifts. They could use a regular human guy like your father to remind them of their human side's abilities. After all, Colonel Owens doesn't have our gifts or anything else magical about him that we know of, and he's a living legend. He's proof of the concept that you don't necessarily have to have magic to be exceptional. It's a good reminder to us all."

They all walked out of the room together. Liam took his leave, as did the captain. Rick parted ways with Wil and Mandy not long after.

"We have about an hour before dinner," Wil said, turning toward Mandy. "Do you want to take a walk?"

A little knot of dread formed in the pit of her stomach. Was this the part where he was going to tell her it was over between them? Not that it had ever had much chance to start, but now that he was back among his peers, she figured their relationship would have to take a backseat. Possibly halt altogether. She was very much afraid it was the latter, based on the serious cast of his features.

Mandy took a deep breath and let it out. "Sure. That sounds nice," she replied, while deep inside, she was already mourning the end of something nascent and beautiful.

Wil wasn't sure how to express the thoughts running through his mind. He wasn't certain of his reception, either. Sure, Mandy had seemed to enjoy their stolen night out of time at the mercenary compound, but now that they were back in his world, he wasn't sure she wanted a repeat performance. Not only that, but he had no idea if she was thinking longer-term than that.

He was, surprisingly enough. Ever since meeting Mandy, his thoughts had strayed to what it might be like to have her in his life on a more permanent basis. Even when he counselled himself to forget such foolishness— because, really, what did he have to offer any woman right now, except uncertainty—he couldn't stop his idle thoughts from turning to the forbidden topic time after time.

Now that he had her on the island, among his unit, he was starting to see a possible future with her in it, and he wanted it. He wanted it badly. More than anything else. He wanted Mandy in his life, in his bed, and in his world, forevermore.

It was a sobering thought. When words like *forever* came up in conjunction with a relationship, he'd always run scared before, but Mandy was different. Something about her calmed him and made him think in terms of forever with joyful anticipation, not fear. She was the only woman he'd ever thought about that way, and he was going to do all he could to convince her to give it a try. That started right now, with this difficult conversation that he wanted to steer into uncharted waters that held things like commitment and feelings that he'd never really fathomed before.

They strolled along the beach. There was a narrow strip of hard-packed sand just beyond the barracks building. It stretched around the island. Wil's unit, and the others on the island, often ran around the circumference of the island both for fitness and to run patrol. The beach was broader and sandier in spots, which made nice places to picnic on days off. There were also, Wil had learned recently, any number of shifters swimming out there, just off the beach, at any given time.

"So, what do you think of the base so far?" he ventured, trying to start the conversation on neutral terms. He wanted to feel her out and see what she was thinking, if he could.

"This island is really nice. It reminds me a little of some of the spots around Seattle, though the weather seems a lot sunnier, so far."

"You grew up in Seattle?" he asked.

Mandy nodded. "Born and raised. Moving to the mountains was a bit of a challenge altitude-wise, at first, but I adjusted. Still, being back at sea level is kind of nice." She lifted her chin and looked out at the water, the breeze blowing her hair back off her face as she breathed deep. "I missed the smell of the ocean."

He breathed a sigh of relief, hearing the truth in her tone. She liked it here. Maybe enough to stay long-term? He'd have to find out.

"That's good," he said, thinking aloud as she looked over at him with a quizzical expression. "I mean, I'm glad you like it here because I was wondering if you'd want to stay a bit longer."

Damn it! Why was he so bad at expressing himself when it really counted? He tried again.

"The thing is… I really like you a lot, and I was hoping you'd want to stay, and we could maybe see where this thing between us might lead." Did that sound cheesy? Gosh, he hoped not.

"I really like you a lot, too," she said quietly, looking down at the sand beneath their feet. Was she blushing? He couldn't tell in the twilight. "But is there a place for me here? I'm not the kind of person who likes to be idle, and this is a military base. It's out of my realm of experience."

"Honestly, this particular base is out of my realm of experience, too," he told her, chuckling a bit. "I don't think there are many like it. This might be the only one, in fact, where magic folk are welcomed and their skills are cultivated." He reached out for her hand as they stopped walking and turned toward each other. "We're allowed to share our secret very sparingly. I shared mine with you."

"Not by choice," she reminded him.

"All the bad guys did was accelerate the timeline," he countered. "I've been thinking about you and trying to find some way to make us work as a couple since almost the moment I met you."

"Seriously?" Her tone indicated doubt, and he was quick to try to erase it.

"Seriously," he replied, looking into her eyes and willing her to see the truth in his gaze. "You intrigued me from the moment we met. There was a connection. A spark. Something I've never felt before and probably never will again. The shifters talk about knowing their fated mates from almost the moment they lay eyes on them. I think I understand that a little better, now. I imagine that's how I felt when I met you, Mandy." Was he getting too serious? He couldn't interpret the change in her expression, but he was afraid he was going too fast and tried to backpedal a little. "Not that we're shifters. I may have this crazy weather ability, now, but I'm still human. I think." He shook his head, as if in doubt.

Mandy started walking again, and he had little choice but to follow her lead. Had he blown it? He wasn't sure.

"You're still human, but you're more," she told him quietly as they walked slowly down the beach. "And you're definitely still in the military. I suspect your commanders have made allowances for Casey and the few other women who live in the barracks, but would that extend to me? I'm not in the military, and I don't plan on joining up anytime soon."

"There are such things as civilian contractors," he told her. "That's the kind of deal they're offering my dad, I think. I might be able to arrange something like that for you."

She stopped short and turned to look at him. "I have no idea what I could possibly do to help a group of super-men." The frustration in her voice was clear, and he realized he'd made a mistake by downplaying her possible contributions.

"Wait. Let's start over," he said, hoping the right words would come to him. "You have undeniable skills, Mandy, and I don't even have to talk to my captain to know that they're already looking into your background to see if there's some way they can entice you to work with us. So few people know about our condition that, when we find an ally, we have generally been signing them on to work more closely with the unit." He shook his head. "I'm not explaining this well, but I'm sure there's a place for you on this base, whether or not we continue as a couple. What I'm asking—or trying to ask—is if you want to be my girlfriend."

"Your girlfriend?" she repeated as if surprised and maybe intrigued. He took heart.

"A childish word for what, I assure you, is a very adult feeling." He moved closer, keeping his tone intimate as he put one arm around her waist and drew her in.

"I like the sound of that." She smiled, rubbing up against him. "I haven't been anybody's girlfriend in ages, but I'd like very much to be yours."

And there, on the beach, with the last rays of the sun shining off the wavelets, he kissed her, and there was no doubt. He felt it in his bones, in his blood, and in his soul. They were made for each other.

Dinner with the unit was a casual affair. Nobody used rank when addressing anyone else, she saw. The captain was simply *Hal*, and the others answered to various nicknames, as well. There were more women than Mandy had expected, peppered around the tables in the dining hall. Hal and Casey had their daughter with them and sat with the man she knew as Jeeves and his wife, Rose.

Rick had been chatting with both couples when Mandy walked in with Wil, but once they had made the rounds of all the tables so Wil could introduce Mandy to everyone, Rick joined them at their table to eat. She thought that was really considerate of him since, of everyone here, she knew Wil and Rick best. It was clear they were all going out of their way to make her feel welcome, which impressed her greatly. This was a nice group of people, and they were extending the hand of friendship to her in a big way that did not go unnoticed or unappreciated.

Another couple joined their table, having arrived after Wil and Mandy. They were introduced as Carter and Hannah. Mandy noticed that Hannah also wore a military uniform and surmised that at least one of the men in the unit had found a girlfriend—as Wil had put it—who was, herself, in the service.

Carter was originally from Portland, Oregon, so he and Mandy compared notes about growing up in the Pacific Northwest. It was a friendly meal shared with interesting people who seemed to be making every effort to make Mandy feel welcome. She appreciated their effort, though she was still in a bit of a daze after all that had happened, and especially her discussion with Wil on the beach. Did she want to be his girlfriend?

You bet your ass she wanted to be his girlfriend. That and so much more. The immediate response that had rung silently through her mind had surprised her in its vehemence. Caught unawares, her subconscious had come out and finally made her realize that she wanted to be with Wil, no matter what. She would never have given herself so freely to a man she didn't care about, and her feelings for Wil grew by leaps and bounds the more she was around him.

She was more than halfway in love with him already, even though they'd only known each other a few days. It didn't seem possible that it should happen so fast. She'd always imagined that falling in love took time and maybe even a little effort, but that was definitely not the case where Wil was concerned.

She had just jumped in with both feet and damned the consequences. She'd fallen hard for the big man, and she still wasn't sure where it would all lead. For now, she felt they'd taken a big step forward. She was his official girlfriend. That had to count for something.

CHAPTER EIGHTEEN

When it was time for bed, Wil led Mandy to his room. They weren't obvious about it, but she could tell he wasn't going to let her sleep in that lonely room to which she'd been assigned. So much the better. She liked the idea of keeping that room as her own space, but after last night, she'd much rather sleep with Wil than all by lonely herself.

When the door to his quarters closed behind them, Mandy looked around with interest. He had a few framed photographs over the desk. One of his dad and himself when they'd both been much younger took prominence, but there were others. Members of his unit in dusty combat gear, posing around some sort of armored vehicle. Another in front of a black helicopter. Yet another aboard a ship. The boys definitely had gotten around.

"This is a bit homier than I expected," she said aloud as she walked into the large room. It was almost the size of a small studio apartment in the city.

"Since coming here, we've been given a lot more leeway as far as personal space goes," Wil told her. "I think it's because they know we're not going anywhere for the foreseeable future. This is home, now." He sighed heavily. "At least until we can figure out exactly who's after us and neutralize the threat. As it is, the Army had someone pack up my off-base apartment and move everything to storage here on the island. All my stuff is in the basement of this building, in fact. It's the same for most of the other guys, too."

"That's rough," Mandy replied, turning toward him. "I put some of my things in storage when I moved to Montana. I wasn't sure I'd like it, so I hesitated before bringing everything out. Plus, I only had the trailer, so I didn't need any furniture, really." She shrugged. "I threw out a lot of stuff before I moved, too, so there wasn't that much left to store. Just the things I really wanted to keep."

"I didn't get a chance to purge before they boxed it all up, so one of the things on my list for my downtime is to sort through the boxes in the basement and clear out the junk. I can also bring a few items up here to make it more like an apartment. Hal not only gave us permission to customize, he encouraged it. Casey thought it was important that we feel at home here, since we won't be leaving anytime soon. She thinks it's good for morale." He gave her a lopsided smile as if such thoughts were foreign to him.

"I can help with the sorting, if you like," she said, bypassing the morale comment. "I got a lot of practice when I was preparing to move."

He came over to her and put one arm around her waist, tugging her close. "I'd appreciate the expert help. Maybe tomorrow we can make a start after work."

"Sounds good," she agreed, moving into his embrace. "I have to earn my keep, you know."

"Ah, about that..." He drew back slightly to meet her gaze. "I had a quick chat with Hal about you. He wants you to meet with him tomorrow morning after breakfast. He has a task in mind for you, if you really want a job."

She eyed him suspiciously. "It's not a make-work thing, right? I don't want or need charity."

"I promise you it's something you are uniquely suited for and that will help us a lot."

"You sound like you know what he's going to propose," she said, squinting up at him. "Spill."

"Oh, Officer, you got me. I can't withstand your brutal interrogation techniques," he quipped, and she tickled his midsection in retaliation. They tussled for a bit, but he captured her hands in his and met her gaze once more. "Okay, it actually has to do with your former position in the police. We've had occasion to interact with local law enforcement on Long Island a few times. The last outing we encountered a shifter detective whose help has been invaluable, but we need a real liaison between our unit and the local LEOs. You speak their language. You'd be ideal for that kind of thing. Hal also mentioned that you had a special interest and strong background in research and investigation. We could use some civilian help on that score, as well, to try to track the paper trail—because there has to be one—of the people that keep coming after us."

Mandy was intrigued. "I always did like the investigative work more than the beat cop stuff," she allowed.

"Well, think about it. Hal will have the particulars of the offer, but I know the Army pays well for civilian consultants. And you could stay here, with me."

She smiled up at him. "And be your girlfriend?"

He nodded, smiling back at her. "I really do like the sound of that."

Wil lowered his head and kissed her. Neither spoke for a long, long time.

After a while, Wil moved them over to the bed. He took off her clothes with painstaking attention to detail, which she appreciated to the fullest. He caressed every inch of skin as he uncovered it and made her writhe in passion before divesting himself of his own clothing with speed and efficiency that left her breathless.

He rejoined her on the bed, coming down over her in a way that made her feel protected and even…cherished. It was a novel feeling in her experience, and the emotion that filled her every time she was near Wil swelled in her breast, filling her heart. The more she was around him, the deeper and fuller the emotion became until it enveloped her being, her very soul.

He joined their bodies with one smooth thrust that brought everything into sharp focus. Passion and desire blossomed and burst into the sky like fireworks on the fourth of July. They strained and strove together, beat matching beat, pulses pounding as they reached for the sky, then exploded together in a fireball of ecstasy that went on and on.

Wil held her for long moments after, spooning her into his warm body and placing them both under the covers on his large bed. She was basking. No other word for it. She felt replete and safe in the arms of a man who was quickly becoming the center of her universe.

"I like this." Wil's sleepy voice came from just behind her as his arm squeezed her waist gently.

"Mm," she agreed. "I do, too." Her eyes had been closed, but they opened at his next words.

"I want this. Forever," he whispered. She rolled to look at him, wanting to be certain she'd heard him correctly. "I really hadn't planned to move this fast. I mean, it was only a few hours ago that I asked you to be my official girlfriend." The smile on his face gave her hope that she hadn't been imagining. "Thing is, even though it's Jeeves who has the far sight, when I think of my future, I can't even imagine it without you. How's that for intense?" He shook his head. "I don't want to scare you off, but at least let me know what you think about that and put me out of my misery, huh?"

She met his gaze, feeling the moisture gathering behind her own eyes. Is this what it felt like to have a dream come true?

"I think that's a really great vision of the future," she told him, laying her heart on the line. "To be honest, I didn't expect I'd ever feel this way about anyone, but you took me by storm." She chuckled a bit at the pun.

Hope grew in his expression. He paused significantly then touched her cheek. "I'm falling in love with you, Mandy." Her heart leapt in joy. "No, scratch that. I'm *in love* with you. Have been since almost the moment we met, though I didn't recognize it at first. Your kindness, your bravery, your intelligence… You drew me to you without even trying."

"I could say the same about you, you know," she replied in a soft voice, her heart filling with the enormity of the love she felt.

"You could?" He looked so hopeful, she took that final, daring step.

She nodded. "I love you, too, Wil. I didn't know I could feel this way or that it could happen so fast, but I feel it, and it feels real."

"Feels pretty damn real to me, too," he agreed, holding her gaze.

"So, what do we do about it?" Mandy asked, breathless.

"Well, right now, the Army is just about

bending over backwards to keep my unit safe and happy. And, since you're key to my happiness, I don't think anyone will object to our relationship. But, just to be sure, I think we should get engaged." His nervous smile belied his casual tone.

"Oh, you think so?" She felt confident enough in his love to tease.

"Yeah, I really do. I want you to be my wife, but I think we need to be at least a little traditional and have an engagement first. Not too long, but maybe long enough to have a party and break it to our friends before we tie the knot. What do you think?"

She felt a little dizzy at the idea of marrying Wil, but nothing had ever sounded so right to her in her life, even if his proposal was a bit non-traditional.

"I think that's one of the best ideas you've ever had," she told him, reaching up to kiss him.

They stayed like that for a very long time, only breaking apart when thunder sounded in the distance. She looked at him warily.

"Did you do that?" she asked, glancing slyly toward the window where they could hear rain was starting to pour down outside.

Wil shook his head. "Sometimes, a storm is just a storm," he protested, but she wasn't buying it. "Of course, the downpour means I won't have to report to the beach at oh-dark-hundred for PT in the morning."

She pushed at his shoulder. "You wouldn't."

He grinned at her. "*Au contraire.* For a few

more minutes with you in my arms, I'd do just about anything." A massive crack of lightning sounded nearby. "It isn't safe for us to run on the beach in a lightning storm." His innocent tone made her giggle.

"Don't you think your captain will get wise to your game?"

"Maybe," he shrugged. "But Hal is a happily married man. I think he'll appreciate a morning, every now and again, when he can sleep-in as much as we will."

The rain pounded down outside with frequent lightning and thunder, but Mandy wasn't afraid. The love of her life was controlling the tempest, and she knew he would never let anything bad happen to her, or his friends on the island. She had never felt safer...or more loved.

# # #

ABOUT THE AUTHOR

Bianca D'Arc has run a laboratory, climbed the corporate ladder in the shark-infested streets of lower Manhattan, studied and taught martial arts, and earned the right to put a whole bunch of letters after her name, but she's always enjoyed writing more than any of her other pursuits. She grew up and still lives on Long Island, where she keeps busy with an extensive garden, several aquariums full of very demanding fish, and writing her favorite genres of paranormal, fantasy and sci-fi romance.

Bianca loves to hear from readers and can be reached through Twitter (@BiancaDArc), Facebook (BiancaDArcAuthor) or through the various links on her website.

WELCOME TO THE D'ARC SIDE…
WWW.BIANCADARC.COM

OTHER BOOKS BY BIANCA D'ARC

Gifts of the Ancients
Warrior's Heart
Future Past
A Friend in Need
Lightning Strikes

Guardians of the Dark
Simon Says
Once Bitten
Smoke on the Water
Night Shade
Shadow Play

Gemini Project
Tag Team
Doubling Down
Deuces Wild

Jaguar Island (Howls)
The Jaguar Tycoon
The Jaguar Bodyguard
The Jaguar's Secret
Baby
The Jaguar Star

Big Wolf
A Touch of Class
Perfect
The Werewolf Alpha's
Solstice Miracle

More Than Mated
The Right Spot

Dragon Knights
*Daughters of the
Dragon*
Maiden Flight*
Border Lair
The Ice Dragon**
Prince of Spies***

The Novellas
The Dragon Healer
Master at Arms
Wings of Change

Sons of Draconia
FireDrake
Dragon Storm
Keeper of the Flame
Hidden Dragons

Sea Captain's Daughter
Sea Dragon
Dragon Fire
Dragon Mates

The Captain's Dragon

PHOENIX RISING

Lance is inexplicably drawn to the sun and doesn't understand why. Tina is a witch who remembers him from their high school days. She'd had a crush on the quiet boy who had an air of magic about him. Reunited by Fate, she wonders if she could be the one to ground him and make him want to stay even after the fire within him claims his soul...if only their love can be strong enough.

PHOENIX AND THE WOLF

Diana is drawn to the sun and dreams of flying, but her elderly grandmother needs her feet firmly on the ground. When Diana's old clunker breaks down in front of a high-end car lot, she seeks help and finds herself ensnared by the sexy werewolf mechanic who runs the repair shop. Stone makes her want to forget all her responsibilities and take a walk on the wild side...with him.

PHOENIX AND THE DRAGON

He's a dragon shapeshifter in search of others like himself. She's a newly transformed phoenix shifter with a lot to learn and bad guys on her trail. Together, they will go on a dazzling adventure into the unknown, and fight against evil folk intent on subduing her immense power and using it for their own ends. They will face untold danger and find love that will last a lifetime.

THE JAGUAR TYCOON

Mark may be the larger-than-life billionaire Alpha of the secretive Jaguar Clan, but he's a pussycat when it comes to the one women destined to be his mate. Shelly is an up-and-coming architect trying to drum up business at an elite dinner party at which Mark is the guest of honor. When shots ring out, the hunt for the gunman brings Mark into Shelly's path and their lives will never be the same.

THE JAGUAR BODYGUARD

Sworn to protect his Clan, Nick heads to Hollywood to keep an eye on a rising star who has seen a little too much for her own good. Unexpectedly fame has made a circus of Sal's life, but when decapitated squirrels show up on her doorstep, she knows she needs professional help. Nick embeds himself in her security squad to keep an eye on her as sparks fly and passions rise between them. Can he keep her safe and prevent her from revealing what she knows?

THE JAGUAR'S SECRET BABY

Hank has never forgotten the wild woman with whom he spent one memorable night. He's dreamed of her for years now, but has never been back to the small airport in Texas owned and run by her werewolf Pack. Tracy was left with a delicious memory of her night in Hank's arms, and a beautiful baby girl who is the light of her life. She chose not to tell Hank about his daughter, but when he finally returns and he discovers the daughter he's never known, he'll do all he can to set things right.

WWW.BIANCADARC.COM

Made in the USA
Columbia, SC
17 June 2021